WHAT
I LIKE ABOUT
Me

WHAT I LIKE ABOUT Me

For my gran, who taught me to love stories.
For my mum, who told me to write my own.
And for Chris, who kept asking for more.

—J. G.

Published by
PEACHTREE PUBLISHING COMPANY INC.
1700 Chattahoochee Avenue
Atlanta, Georgia 30318-2112
www.peachtree-online.com

Text © 2019 by Jenna Guillaume

First published in Australia in 2019 by Pan Macmillan Australia Pty Ltd
1 Market Street, Sydney, New South Wales, Australia, 2000
First United States version published in 2020 by Peachtree Publishing Company Inc.

Printed in February 2020 in the United States of America by LSC Communications
in Harrisonburg, VA
10 9 8 7 6 5 4 3 2 1
First Edition
ISBN: 978-1-68263-160-7

Cataloging-in-Publication Data is available from the Library of Congress.

WHAT I LIKE ABOUT me

JENNA GUILLAUME

PEACHTREE

ATLANTA

Friday, 15 December

3 things I discovered today:

1. Ms. Singh is a sadistic sumbitch who thinks it's a great idea to assign homework over vacation.

Evidence: This journal, which I'm supposed to write my "discoveries" in every damn day, complete with evidence of source material and explanatory notes— like I have so much time for that. All because my English teacher thinks school should be about "so much more than prescribed texts." As though forcing teenagers to keep a "discovery journal" is gonna teach us profound life lessons, like some carpe bloody diem crap, when really the only thing we want to discover is each other's bodies.

2. Growing up bites the big one, if this is the kind of BS you have to put up with.

Evidence: When I whinged about this homework to Mum, she rolled her eyes and said that committing to responsibilities is a part of growing up: "Look at your father, working his butt off while you're relaxing yours on the beach."

Which is profoundly annoying for several reasons: the first being that Mum and Dad have been arguing nonstop about Dad working through our vacation, so it's not like she's happy about it; the second being that I can't even vent without Mum getting a dig in about my "tendency to give up when things get difficult;" and the third being that it's not as if writing in this thing every day OVER VACATION is actually a responsibility that matters, like it's going to change my life, and when I'm an adult and living on my own I'm going to get to the end of each day, sit down with my glass of wine and handwrite in a Moleskin notebook: "Dear Diary, today I discovered that the college degree I spent four years and $40,000 on is absolutely useless and never going to get me a job, so I guess I'm going to become a checkout chick at the supermarket after all." Yeah. Right.

3. If you find an eleven-month-old packet of Milk Duds in your suitcase, it's really not a good idea to eat it.

Evidence: Uh...you're just going to have to trust me on this one.

* * *

I'm never actually going to hand this in. Can you imagine?

"Oh, Maisie, I really liked the part where you called me a sadistic sumbitch; you showed some deep insight there. Forget about doing coursework for the rest of the year, because this is so damn good you're getting full marks on *everything*." —Ms. Singh, never.

"Maisie Martin, you are on afternoon detention for the rest of the year, and your mother is getting a phone call." —Ms. Singh, probably.

But honestly, after all the crap adults give you about appreciating your youth and embracing the best years of your life and blah blah blah, do they actually help you to do that? No. It's:

"Maisie, you've got to do this homework!"

"Maisie, this year will decide your future!"

"Maisie, should you really be eating that?"

"Maisie, I can't come to Cobbers Bay this time, and you're going to spend three weeks without an ally against your mother, who is perpetually disappointed in you, and your sister, who thinks she's much better than you, and your sister's new girl-friend, who is probably even more perfect than she is, and life's a bitch and then you die."

Okay, so my dad didn't really say that last bit, just the bit about not coming to the Bay, but he may as well have said the rest. He's breaking a fourteen-year tradition, all because the newspaper he works for decided to launch some "digital rebranding strategy" in the new year, and so he won't be getting a month off like he normally does. It's just complete garbage if you ask me. (Which no one ever does.)

At least one good thing came out of Dad ditching me: Mum's letting my brilliant, beautiful, best-friend-in-the-world Anna come to "keep me company" (translation: keep me quiet). Anna also got ditched by a parent for the holidays (her mum is going overseas with her boyfriend), PLUS she happened to have her heart broken last week, so it worked out great.

Wait, that came out wrong... What I meant to say was, Anna needs a distraction because she's upset with her mum and she doesn't talk to her dad and she found out via *text message* that her (now ex-) boyfriend, Dan the Dickhead, was cheating on her. Luckily I, her most excellent best friend, am able to provide an all-expenses-paid trip to a luxury resort in an idyllic, sunny seaside town. (Okay, it's not a luxury resort—more like a two-bedroom cabin in a cheesy RV park—but the rest is basically true.) It's win-win really, because Anna gets her distraction and I get my ally. Except for the part where Anna is heartbroken; that's less "win" and more "complete suckage." But I'll put her back together again, even if it takes me this entire vacation.

Which means I'm NOT going to write in this ridiculous journal every day. I'm only doing it right now because

a) Mum told me she wants to see that I've done it before bed, and

b) it beats packing, which I'm also supposed to be doing. But anything beats packing.

Ugh. I really should pack.

Bye, Discovery Journal. I'd say you were good while you lasted, but that would be a lie and I really try never to lie. At least, not to inanimate objects.

Saturday, 16 December

1 thing I discovered today:

1. My mother is a hell demon determined to destroy my life.

Evidence: She's actually going to make me write in this bloody journal every day. She said she's going to check it every morning! WHILE WE'RE ON VACATION. This is what happens when your mum is a teacher. She always sides with her own kind. Oh, she's promised not to read what I write, just confirm that I have written *something*, like that makes her a saint instead of a hell demon. But I know her true form, and it breathes fire. And because I don't plan on being burned by anything other than the sun, I'll have to do as she says. That doesn't mean I'm going to write anything worth handing in, though. Ha ha! I'll show my mother *and* Ms. Singh in one foul swoop. (Fowl swoop? Fell swoop?!)

* * *

Hi, Discovery Journal. Fancy meeting you again. Yeah. I didn't think this would happen either. I thought we were kaput. Dunzo. Finished. But my mother has other ideas, and I used up a lifetime's worth of defying her in a single act (ONE FELL SWOOP?!) when I quit dancing, so I'm essentially doomed to do whatever she says until I'm at least eighty-four years old or she dies, whichever comes first. (My money is on the former; my mother, as I have already mentioned, is a hell demon and will probably live forever.)

But I'm a guerrilla freedom fighter (NOT gorilla, which I learned the hard way in history last year, whoops), and I can resist in my own small ways. For example, my mother told me I have to write in this book every day, but she didn't tell me what to write. Therefore I will now fill it with utter nonsense. Watch me go.

Blah blah blah blah blah blah blah blah blah blah blah blah di blah blah blah blah blah lalala lalala lalalala my hand is getting kind of tired to be honest blah blah blah blah blah blah.

Mum is watching me. She thinks I'm actually doing my homework. Ha ha! Hahahahahaha!

And the crowd goes wild! *Clap clap clap clap*... Hey, remember that rhyme?

My mother, your mother lives down the street, 18/19 Marble Street, and every night they have a fight and this is what they say: "Girls are sexy made out of Pepsi, boys are rotten made out of cotton."

Question: how does being made out of Pepsi make one sexy? Because I have drunk my fair share of Pepsi, and let me tell you, I am most definitely not what you'd call sexy. Anna, on the other hand, never touches the stuff and she is a certified Hot Girl™. You know: the kind of girl who oozes sexiness, who drips confidence, who makes guys do that cartoon eyes-popping-out-of-their-heads-tongues-falling-out-of-their-mouths thing whenever she walks past, who is just so completely *herself* and has a killer face and a rockin' bod to boot. Don't ask me why she's friends with me. I'm basically the exact opposite of a Hot Girl™, despite the fact I was birthed by a Hot Girl™, who had already birthed another Hot Girl™, and then somehow wound up with me. It's like in that old movie *Twins*, which I've watched with Dad a hundred times, where Arnold Schwarzenegger gets all the good genes and Danny DeVito is the leftover sludge. My sister, Eva, is Arnold Schwarzenegger and I'm the DeVito sludge.

Anyway. Blah blah blah blah blah blah blah blah blah blah blah blah blah blah blah blah blah blah

blah blah blah blah blah blah blah blah blah blah blah blah blah blah blah blah blah blah blah blah blah blah blah blah blah blah blah blah blah blah blah blah blah blah blah blah blah blah blah blah blah blah blah blah blah blah blah blah blah.

That should do it.

Sunday, 17 December

2 things I discovered today:

1. I'm not as good at guerrilla freedom fighting as I thought I was.

Evidence: All those "blahs" yesterday caught Mum's eye, and she threatened to read this whole journal cover to cover if I didn't start taking it seriously. "Privacy comes with trust, and you have to earn trust, Maisie. And don't roll your eyes at me." *insert eye roll here* Anyway, I have to stop with the nonsense and at least *look* like I'm doing this properly. So the substance can be nonsense, just not the form. Hey, look, I'm getting better at this already.

2. You know all those movies where teenagers have, like, THE TIME OF THEIR LIVES? This vacation is probably not going to be that.

Evidence: Everything that has happened since yesterday.

* * *

Here we are again, Discovery Journal! Can I call you DJ, since we're going to be *such* good friends and all? You can call me Maisie. Some people call me Maise, pronounced 'maze,' because I'm totally a puzzle you need to explore before you can get to the treasure hidden inside. Okay, that's not true—it's just short for Maisie, duh. Mum calls me Missy-May, god knows why, and Dad calls me Eminem, because he thinks he's hilarious. (Don't tell him, but he kinda is sometimes.) You know what? Call me whatever you want. Or, better yet, don't call me anything, because you're an empty journal and can't actually speak.

Of course, I could fill you with words that would certainly enable you to say something.

But what should those words be?! As aforementioned (a great word to use in any assignment to give the impression you know what you're talking about, btw), Mum cottoned on to my cunning plan yesterday. Which means today has to be different. I guess I could go into the also-aforementioned Everything That Has Happened Since Yesterday. That'd take up some space alright.

To start with, most of yesterday was pretty boring. We were in the car for a lot of the day—Mum, Anna, and I. (Eva's flying up from Melbourne, where she's studying dance—like she hasn't already been doing that her whole damn life. She'll arrive in a few days with her new girlfriend, Bess. Just my luck they're not spending Christmas with *her* family.) Anyway, we were in the car for hours and hours, and Mum kept trying to talk to us about school and the future and, worst of all, boys, so Anna put her earphones in and pretended to be asleep, while I just shot Mum death stares until she stopped talking and started sending me death stares back.

We're pretty good at speaking in death stares. Here's the rough translation:

Me: *Mum, stop trying to talk to us like you're our friend. You're not our friend.*

Mum: *I'm trying to make everyone comfortable.*

Me: *Well you're making everyone UNcomfortable.*

Mum: *Don't be so disrespectful, Maisie Martin. If you carry on behaving like this I'll lock you in the cabin, and you won't get to have any fun.*

Me: *I dare you to do just that. It'd be lovely, to be honest. I could watch Netflix all day.*

Mum: *I have just now realized that you would love that, and have decided a more fitting punishment would be to force you to stay by my side this entire vacation and never let you out of my sight. Hey, we could get bikini waxes together! Perfect!*

Me: *You wouldn't.*

Mum: *I would.*

Me: . . .

Mum: . . .

Me: *looks away, defeated*

Mum: *smiles smugly, victorious*

Anna: *snores because she is no longer pretending to be asleep and now really is asleep*

Yeah. That's pretty much how the eight-hour car ride went. Dad messaged a few times along the way to say he was missing us already and he wished he was there. It just made Mum swear under her breath.

Then we reached the Bay and things went from boring to a little too exciting all at once. And by exciting, I mean absolutely mortifying.

Anna, looking adorably bedraggled after the long trip—as opposed to me, who looked bedraggled in the sense that I resembled something that had been caught in the wheel and dragged along behind the car the whole time—headed straight inside with her bag. I helped Mum unload the kitchen sink and various other supplies she'd insisted on bringing (not literally the kitchen sink, though it may as well have been—Mum's mantra is "always be prepared," but she brought so many water bottles along it's like she's a doomsday prepper). Once Mum was occupied putting everything in just the right place in the cabin, I went back out to get my own bag. By this stage, Anna had already dumped her stuff on the top bunk in the little room we're sharing and was now sitting on the table on the veranda, staring past the row of cabins in front of ours to the ocean. I cracked a joke about Mum's excessiveness, but Anna didn't even crack a smile. She'd been in a bad mood all day, and it seemed it was going to take something drastic to lift it.

When I saw the box of tampons next to my bag in the trunk of the car, I got an idea. It seemed brilliant at the time, but it was probably the silliest I've ever had, and that's saying something.

(I can't believe I'm going to write this down.)

Hidden from Anna's view by the open trunk, I opened the box and retrieved two tampons.

(Oh god, I wish I could turn back time.)

I shoved one tampon in my nostril.

(Why why *why* did I do this?!)

I shoved the other tampon in my other nostril.

(Oh please, won't some lightning strike me dead on the spot?)

I cackled wildly.

(It all happened so fast.)

I ran around the car toward Anna.

(And yet it was somehow also in slow motion.)

"Hey, Annaaaaa," I sing-songed to get her attention.

(I'm dying, I'm dying.)

I blew out really hard through my nose, and one tampon went flying.

(I'm dead.)

I froze, one tampon still in my nose, as I watched the other ricochet off the beautiful, perfect arm of none other than Sebastian Lee.

(Here lies Maisie Martin, dead from embarrassment, aged sixteen.)

I need a moment.

* * *

Okay, I'm back. My whole body is cringing, but I'm here. I may as well see this thing through.

Where was I? Oh right, the most humiliating moment of my life. The Tampon Incident, starring Sebastian Lee and my cold, dead corpse.

The thing about Sebastian Lee is he's the most beautiful guy you'll ever see. He's got this glorious dark hair that you just want to reach out and touch, and this incredible jawline that you just want to reach out and touch, and these spectacular shoulders that you just want to reach out and touch, and...well, you get the picture.

The other thing about Sebastian Lee is I've known him my whole life. Our mums did their teaching degrees together and have been besties ever since, but they don't get to see each other much, because the Lees moved to Queensland when I was two and we stayed in New South Wales. Mum and Laura made a pact to spend their vacations together every year, and that's how each family wound up with a cabin in Cobbers Bay. Which is how Sebastian and I ended up spending vacation after vacation swimming naked together and boogie boarding and building sand-castles and playing *Star Wars* (he was Han Solo, I was Chewbacca...also I should note the naked part stopped when we were, like, four...damn). We always had fun, no matter what we were doing. Sebastian could turn anything into a game.

Well, not anything. That makes him sound kinda shallow, which he's not. He knows how to be serious too. Even when we were kids, he was a good listener. I remember this one time when I was ten, I was upset because Greer Kirkpatrick had given everyone at school Christmas cards except for me. Sebastian let me cry about it, and he didn't laugh once. Instead, he got this little crease in between his eyebrows, and he said that if he ever met this Greer Kirkpatrick, he'd kick dirt straight into her no-good, card-hogging face. The next day, underneath my pillow, I found a handmade Christmas card covered in pink glitter, signed from my "secret Santa." I knew it was from him.

Because that's the other thing about Sebastian Lee. He's sensitive and thoughtful—far more than most people realize. I didn't even fully understand it myself until I read his poetry. He doesn't know about that little fact, of course. It happened a few years back, when I was looking for insect repellent inside the Lees' cabin. Everyone else was outside, and Sebastian's bedroom door just *happened* to be open and his notebook just *happened* to be on his bed, so I just *happened* to wander in and take a peek. What I saw was his soul. And it touched mine.

Which brings me to one final thing about Sebastian Lee: I've been in love with him since I was thirteen years old. Probably earlier. It was the poetry that really pushed me over the edge, though. I felt like I was carrying around this private, beautiful part of him. Like I was closer to him than ever before. Ironically, we'd kinda drifted apart by then. His mate Beamer had started coming on vacation with the Lees, and

Sebastian was always off with him. When we were together, I got real awkward. Not that he seemed to notice. At least, he didn't say anything about it. He didn't say much to me from there on out, actually. But it went both ways. Like I said, I was awkward. I *am* awkward. Can't-form-a-coherent-sentence-and-instead-communicate-solely-in-squeaks level awkward.

Just like the squeak I let out yesterday when I saw the tampon that had been in my nose seconds before it hit Sebastian's beautiful, perfect arm.

It turns out he had walked up to our cabin from his family's about the time I was shoving tampons in my nostrils. He had reached Anna just as I was running around the car, screaming like a drunken lemur. He was looking at me with wide eyes right around the time the tampon hit his beautiful, perfect arm. It all happened in the space of about ten seconds. That's all the time it takes to destroy your life.

Anna was also staring at me with wide eyes and a mouth to match. She was the first of us to speak.

"Maisie, what are you doing?"

I opened my mouth but all that came out was one of those prolonged squeaks.

And then. AND THEN.

Sebastian Lee reached his beautiful, perfect arm

down to the ground and plucked that tampon up by its string. Sebastian Lee held out his beautiful, perfect arm with that tampon dangling at the end, and said, "I think you dropped something, Maisie."

And then. AND THEN.

He cracked up. And Anna cracked up. And Anna casually put her hand on his beautiful, perfect arm.

Just like that. Like she was the one who'd known him her whole life, when they'd just met ninety seconds before.

I tried to muster up a laugh myself. Just more squeaking. Apparently that reminded Sebastian Lee why he was standing in front of our cabin in the first place.

"Hey, Dad wanted me to see if you guys were up for dinner tonight? He's staked out the grill."

"Seb! How are you, love?" Suddenly Mum was there, wiping her hands on a tea towel and giving Sebastian a kiss on the cheek. "That sounds great. Tell your dad we'll be there in about half an—Maisie, what on earth are you doing? Get that thing out of your nose!"

Oh. Yeah. I still had a tampon in one nostril. I hastily yanked it out. Sebastian Lee shook his head and let out a breath that sounded like it would have been a laugh if he could be bothered to make it one.

"Cool. Well. Catch youse later." He walked away and

I watched him go, feeling like if I died right then and there I wouldn't even be mad—I'd be grateful.

I turned back to Mum and Anna, who were both shaking their heads too.

Yeah. The trip got off to a GREAT start.

* * *

We were late to the barbecue because Anna couldn't decide what to wear. I'd changed out of the tights and T-shirt I'd worn for the drive into...fresh tights and a T-shirt. Meanwhile, Anna was on her fourth outfit change.

"That looks awesome," I said as she rolled her eyes and peeled off the crop top she'd paired with tiny denim shorts.

"Ugh, I feel so fat," she said, grabbing at her taut stomach and pulling a face.

"C'mon, it's just a family barbecue. Who cares what you wear?" I said, trying to ignore the familiar twist in my gut I get whenever Anna puts herself down like that. She just looked at me the way she does sometimes, like I'm an alien from outer space who can't speak any Earth language, let alone English. I sighed and bent down to pluck a yellow dress from the pile of clothes she'd dumped on the floor.

"Here, put this on, you always feel good in it," I said. I was relieved when she declared it "would do." If there's one thing my mum hates (in fact there are many things she hates but, you know, it's a figure of speech), it's lateness. She'd already grown tired of waiting and left without us, having freshened up and got herself looking like a million bucks in under twenty minutes. She's the master of the quick change, my mum.

And the quick drink. She was on her second glass of wine by the time we got there. I know this because she said, "Took you girls long enough; I'm already on my second glass of wine."

I said hi to Sebastian's parents and his brothers, Kane and Lincoln, (they're twins, and they used to be really cute, but now they're eleven and just massive pests, so I avoid them as much as possible). I carefully and very deliberately avoided all eye contact with Sebastian Lee himself. Which was much less successful than it usually is, because he came straight over to talk to us.

"How's it goin'? Anna, right? We didn't really meet properly before."

She laughed, and I quietly died inside all over again as the image of that tampon hitting Sebastian Lee's beautiful, perfect arm flashed in my head.

"I know," Anna said. "I can't believe I'm finally in the presence of the famous Sebastian Lee."

"Famous?"

"Oh, Maisie never stops talking about you. I've been waiting for this day for years. Ouch, Maise, why are you pinching me?"

Sebastian had this expression on his face, which I would have described as "bemused," but Ms. Singh spent a good twenty minutes lecturing us in class last term about how everyone misunderstands that word and that it actually means *puzzled* or *confused*. She said the decline of the English language made her want to sit down on the ground and weep (and don't even get her started on those "dreadful slang words" we all use). Meanwhile, I was contemplating whether *I* could get away with sitting down on the ground and weeping right there in front of Anna and Sebastian, when I got a strong whiff of BO and felt a heavy arm land across my shoulders.

"Well if it isn't Maisie Martin." Beamer. Ugh. "How's your Aunt Flo?"

"I don't have an Aunt Flo," I started to say, but the smirk on his face suddenly made it click. The Tampon Incident. Sebastian had told him. The day really couldn't get any worse.

Except, of course, it could.

Here's the thing about Beamer: apparently he gets off on annoying me. Like last year, he attacked me with a water gun on one of the few days I ventured to the beach, when I very clearly didn't want to get wet. Two years ago, he kept flicking his eyelids inside out like boys used to do in primary school, because he knew it freaked me out. At least it was an improvement on the times he used to *pick his nose and flick it my way.* The first time he came here, he seized every opportunity he could to snap the straps of my swimsuit. In short, he is a disgusting, infuriating, grade-A pain in my butt.

So of course he barely left my side all night. I guess he's realized his mere presence makes my blood boil, and that's his new tactic. When I pulled up a chair for Anna to sit next to me while we ate, Beamer said, "Aw, thanks, Maisie Martin, you shouldn't have," and plonked himself down in it. He (deliberately) didn't get the hint when I said, "I didn't," so Sebastian carried two more chairs over to form a little circle with the four of us.

It would have been kinda nice, except Beamer didn't stop talking. He launched into a monologue about the brilliance of the latest *Fast and the Furious* movie (which I happened to like, but I wasn't going to let him know that), and didn't let up for a good ten minutes. I shouldn't complain, really, because it did give me the chance to inspect Sebastian up close without it being weird. As Beamer droned on, the rest of us ate, rolled our eyes (mainly me), occasionally laughed (mainly Sebastian), and I kept sneaking glances. At Sebastian, I mean. Not at Beamer. Blech.

I noticed that Sebastian seems to have grown taller since last year. His shoulders are broader, and his hair's a little longer too. Somehow, he's even more gorgeous. As always, he wore a lazy sort of half-smile on his face. It's his default expression. You know how there's Resting Bitch Face? Well, Sebastian Lee has Resting Dreamy Face.

I watched as he worked his way meticulously around his plate. He ate food by food, saving his dad's satay skewers—his favorite, since we were kids—until last. I asked him once when we were younger why he always ate the best food last, instead of gobbling it down first like I did. He'd grinned and said, "That means it's the flavor that stays in my mouth at the end. It's worth the wait, Maise."

Worth the wait. Maybe that's what I'd be to him too. Sebastian was all about delayed gratification. I could get behind some gratification myself, as long as Sebastian Lee was involved. After all these years, maybe—

"What's that little smile of yours about, eh, Maisie Martin?" Beamer's voice broke into my thoughts.

I looked up, startled, and realized everyone was looking at me expectantly.

I turned to Beamer, playing up the sweet smile on my face, and said, "Oh, I was just thinking about the thousand and one ways I could cause you grievous bodily harm with this fork."

He nearly choked on his ginger beer, but his coughing quickly gave way to laughter. "She's quite the kinky one, isn't she?"

I felt my face heat up. I glanced over at Sebastian, who was chuckling and shaking his head. When he noticed me looking, he rolled his eyes, as if to say, "This guy, am I right?" I grinned in return, and a beat passed in which it felt like everyone and everything around us fell away, and it was just the two of us sitting there.

Then Beamer broke in once again. "Anyway, as I was saying, The Rock—"

"Oh my *god*, don't you ever shut up?" Anna said. She was smiling, but I knew Beamer was annoying her already. She's not my best friend for nothing, you know.

Sebastian laughed and said, "He doesn't, actually. He even talks in his sleep. I barely get a moment's rest when we're here."

"Ah, you love it," Beamer fired back.

"Why *are* you here, anyway?" Anna asked him. "Were you abandoned like me, or what?"

I reflexively sucked in a breath and glanced at Beamer. Anna's words were a bit too close to the truth. Beamer's never talked much about his life, but from what I've overheard, it's like this: deadshit dad, drug addict mum, grandad died when he was nine, older sister pissed off overseas, leaving Beamer alone with his gran. And the Lees.

"It gives his grandmother a break, poor woman," I heard Laura telling my mum when they first brought him to the Bay. She'd need one, having to put up with Beamer all the time.

I probably shouldn't say things like that. But I mean really. He is The Worst. Anyway, he just brushed off Anna's comment with a "something like that" and went back to talking about exploding cars. He was fine.

I heard Sebastian say to Anna quietly, "What do you mean, you were abandoned?" And she leaned in close to him and, I presume, told him about her mum's obsession with her new boyfriend and how she, Anna, hasn't seen her dad since she was little. Maybe she even got on to the subject of Dan the Dickhead. I don't know, because all I could hear was

Beamer's foolish opinions about The Rock. (He said he was the greatest action hero of all time, which is ABSURD. But what's even more absurd is that I took the bait and ended up arguing with him for twenty minutes about why there'll never be anyone greater than Arnold Schwarzenegger. So, who's the real fool here?)

By that stage Mum was on to her second *bottle* of wine and had got up and started dancing, lifting her skirt at the sides in the way she only does when she's really drunk, to the whooping and cheering of Sebastian's parents and even Beamer (ugh).

"Go, Mrs M!" he called out to her. To me he said, "Your mum's a bit of a milf, hey."

Which officially tipped me over my Beamer Tolerance Threshold. Anna was still deep in conversation with Sebastian, who was listening intently, that adorable little crease having made an appearance in between his eyebrows. I suddenly felt a bit ill. I got up and sat next to Sebastian's dad.

I like Jimmy. He's okay—you know, for a parent. He makes terrible dad jokes all the time, but he's also a total romantic. He came here from Malaysia to study in the nineties and ended up marrying Laura. One time, at a barbecue not unlike this one, when Mum was (of course) dancing, and Laura was dancing with her, I was sitting quietly between Jimmy and my dad. They'd had a few to drink, and I think they forgot I was there. They were watching their wives dance. Jimmy got this expression on his face that's hard to describe. You know that scene in, like, every romantic comedy, where the girl is looking at a glorious view and says something like, "This is the most beautiful thing I've ever seen," and the guy says, "I know," but he's not looking at the view at all—he's really looking at her? Well, it was like that. Without taking his eyes off Laura, Jimmy said to my dad, "You know, mate, I fell in love with her the moment I saw her." And my dad said, "I know, mate." And something inside me ached, because I'd *never* seen him look at my mum like that.

Dad's not like Jimmy. I don't think he has a romantic bone in his body. He doesn't like to talk about his feelings or make grand gestures. His love is quiet. But it's there. I know it is.

I think…

No, I know.

I do wonder sometimes if my mum sees it, though. If she feels it. He seems to piss her off more than anything. Especially lately.

I was thinking about this as I sat there with Jimmy, half-listening to him talk about how much it sucked that Dad hadn't been able to come this year.

"Still, at least he's working instead of being laid off like half his colleagues, eh?" Jimmy said.

"Yeah," I agreed, but there was something else I wanted to say. "Hey, Jimmy?"

"Hey, Maisie!" He laughed at his own "joke."

I hesitated for a moment, but I couldn't keep the thought in any longer. "Do you think my parents are happy together?"

He looked surprised. He glanced up at Mum, who had dragged Laura up to dance with her, both of them pissing themselves laughing. "Yeah, Maisie. I think they are." He looked back at me. "Why do you ask? Everything alright at home?"

"Yeah," I said. "I'm just being weird. Forget it."

He smiled and ruffled my hair the way he has done since I was a little kid. Usually it annoys me. This time, it didn't. This time, it made me want to keep talking. About how everything isn't alright at home. About how lately, when Mum and Dad aren't arguing, they're barely talking to each other. About how I'm trying not to notice it, trying not to think about it. About how deep down, it really scares me.

But then Beamer was running past us, Kane and Lincoln following close behind, all of them yelling and laughing. And the moment was broken. The twins caught up to Beamer and tackled him to the ground, hooting in delight. Jimmy got up to join them in a game of hide and seek, and I reluctantly agreed to play too.

Meanwhile, Anna and Sebastian just kept talking and talking. I think she spoke more to him in one night than I have in years.

And as I crouched in the shadows, hiding from Beamer, who was "it," a long-held fantasy of Sebastian looking at me the way Jimmy had looked at Laura that time—like I might be the most glorious view he's ever seen—floated into my head. And I felt it slip away.

Later, when I asked Anna what she and Sebastian were talking about for so long, she said, "Oh, you know, just stuff. Nothing special." Then she said, "Maisie, you told me he was hot, but you didn't tell me he was *that* hot."

And I laughed. But I really wanted to cry.

* * *

Gosh that sounds mopey, doesn't it? I've gotta snap out of it. Because you know who's not mopey? Anna! My best friend, who has been mopey for weeks! The trip is working!

But...I think it's because of Sebastian. And a part of me...a selfish part of me...wishes it wasn't.

Because yeah. Today happened. This morning, it was Anna's turn to get annoyed at *me* for taking too long to get ready. Not because I wanted to look particularly special. I just wanted to look something other than awful.

There I go being mopey again. But you see, DJ, I have one swimsuit that fits me. It's a black one-piece, and it makes my boobs look saggy. I hate it. I ended up putting an old pair of my dad's board shorts and a big, loose t-shirt over the top of it. Fat chance (ha!) I'd be going swimming, anyway. Next to Anna in her tiny string bikini (Hot Girl™ approved), I actually felt like the sasquatch some of the guys at school call me. For a moment I questioned why I had even invited her. Because I'm a terrible friend.

Then again, it's not like I look any better on my own. I usually avoid the beach, which is not exactly easy to do in this place, but my family has mostly given up on trying to get me out, and I think Dad secretly likes it because it gives him an excuse to hang out and watch movies with me half the time. Which just makes Mum more annoyed. The look of excitement on her face when I told her where we were headed today almost made me turn around and go straight back to bed. But making Anna happy took priority. SEE? I'm not so terrible...right?

We hit the beach and spent ten minutes trying to find the perfect spot according to Anna's exacting standards. I saw Sebastian and Beamer's familiar old towels lying in the sand, and Anna decided that *they* had found the perfect spot and we should definitely crash it. I felt exactly how I always feel when the prospect of Sebastian Lee looms on the horizon: simultaneously thrilled and so nervous I wanted to vomit.

We laid our towels on the sand and sat down facing the water. Anna started spreading sunscreen on her legs. I told her she should have applied it while she was waiting for me, since you're supposed to put it on at least twenty minutes before going in the sun. She rolled her eyes and told me to chill, which was literally impossible for me to do at that point in time, because Sebastian Lee was heading toward us. Dripping with water, glistening in the sun. Everything felt like it was in slo-mo again, although unlike the Tampon Incident, it was aaallllll good (nervous stomach pains notwithstanding). He semi-jogged up the beach, a smile on his face and his muscles on full display, a picture so hot it could make a nun forget her vows. I could just about hear a cheesy pop song playing over the top of the scene, imploring me to kiss him...*record scratch*

Me: "Beamer! YOU'RE GETTING ME ALL WET!"

Beamer: "Jeez, Maisie, take a guy out for dinner first, will ya?"

Anna: "Seb, will you spread this cream on my back?"

Beamer: "Jeez, Anna, take a guy out for dinner first, will ya?"

Sebastian: "Beamer!"

Anna: "Seb?"

Me: "Anna?"

Beamer: "Maisie!"

Me: "Beamer!"

While I was busy exchanging insults with Beamer, Sebastian spread sunscreen all over Anna's back, and they were soon heading into the water. Beamer asked if I wanted to go in too, but I just put my earphones in, hoping he'd get the hint and leave me alone. I forgot who I was dealing with. He grabbed my phone, ripping the earphones out of my ears along with it and putting them in his own.

"Whatcha listening to?"

Something as dark as my heart.

"Hff. No wonder you look miserable, listening to this emo shit."

I'm miserable because you won't leave me alone.

"That's better!" Beamer unplugged my earphones and played his selection out loud. It was, of all things, Taylor Swift.

"Aw, Beamer. I didn't peg you for a Swiftie," I said.

"I'm a man of many surprises, Maisie Martin," he said. And then he started dancing. Right there on the beach. He was surprising, alright. He was also really bad.

"What are you doing?!" I looked around. No one was really paying attention, thankfully. It was still embarrassing. "Beamer, stop!"

He was dancing in circles around me, tucking his elbows in and flapping his arms. Oh god. He wasn't just dancing. He was doing the *chicken dance*.

"Come on, Maisie, I know you want to dance!"

He reached down to grab my hands, swinging them back and forth.

"I don't dance!" I said, pulling away from him.

He paused and started to say something, but at that moment a strange girl danced up—I'm not kidding—*danced up* next to him, singing along to the song. Now, she was actually pretty good. She had rhythm, at least. Beamer looked at her for a second, and started dancing again himself. He was still bad. The girl didn't seem to care. They faced each other and she started mimicking his awful moves. They were both laughing. It almost made me want to laugh too. Almost.

The song ended and an "emo shit" one started. I reached up, grabbed my phone out of Beamer's hand, and turned the music off.

"Hey, the party was just getting started," the strange girl said.

"Do you two know each other?"

"Nup," Beamer said, raising his chin in the strange girl's direction. "Beamer—nice to meetcha."

"I'm Leila," the girl replied, with one of the most beautiful smiles I've ever seen.

"This here's Maisie Martin."

"I can speak for myself, thanks, Beamer."

"Of course you can, girl!" Leila said, sitting down on Anna's towel next to me.

Beamer went and grabbed his and Sebastian's stuff from nearby and then stretched out on his towel on the other side of me.

Leila grinned at us. "Well. Tell me your life stories!"

I just stared at her.

Beamer snorted. "Not much to tell."

"Beamer lives with his gran," I volunteered, and then immediately regretted it. It felt like a betrayal, although of what I don't know.

"Maisie's a dancer," Beamer blurted out.

I shot him a sharp look, but his face remained placid.

Leila laughed. It was a great laugh.

"And here I was thinking you were the dancer around here," she said to him. I laughed at that, and she looked at me. "So why weren't you dancing just now? I was lying over there just casually minding my own business when I saw this guy making a fool of himself and I thought, he's in desperate need of some backup. But you were here the whole time. I shouldn't have interrupted. Sorry. You guys just looked like fun."

"Oh...no, it's totally fine!" I said, at the same time as Beamer said, "We *are* fun!"

"So why weren't you dancing?" Leila persisted.

"We're at the beach, for one thing," I said.

"And?"

"And...I don't dance anymore."

"What do you mean?"

Jeez, she didn't stop. I wanted to kill Beamer. I looked at him, hoping he'd bail me out of the mess he'd created. He just raised his eyebrows, the picture of innocence, and said, "Yeah, what do you mean? I thought you loved dancing."

I sighed. Because what he said was true. I loved dancing. *Loved*, as in past tense. I mean, it was hard to do otherwise when I was a kid. Mum had me and Eva dancing practically before we could walk. Jazz, ballet, tap...you name it, we learned it. Mum had always dreamed of being a dancer herself, but her parents didn't have the money or care factor to get her any kind of lessons. I reckon half the reason she had kids was because she wanted to be the opposite kind of parent. An actual Dance Mom.

It worked out with Eva, the perfect little dancer who happily attended classes every day of the week and gave up her weekends to training and competitions and more training. It didn't work out so well with me. Instead of Eva 2.0, Mum got lumped with a far-from-perfect kid who was just never good enough, no matter how hard I tried. And boy, did I try. Until one day it wasn't remotely fun anymore. And I stopped trying. And then I stopped dancing altogether. At first, Mum tried to force it—"Think of your health! Your confidence!"—but eventually she gave up, finally recognizing I was a lost cause. Which meant Mum could devote *all* her time and energy into Eva and her oh-so-promising talent, without having to give me a second thought. They should have thanked me, really.

Leila and Beamer were both looking at me expectantly. "I got over it," I said. I turned to Leila. "What's your story, then?"

She smiled. "Well, I've lived here my whole life. My parents own a B&B just up the road. I help Mum in the mornings and the rest of the day I'm off the hook. I spend a lot of time working on my designs, but I needed some inspiration today. I want to be a designer, you know? I make my own clothes. I made this! What do you think?"

Over her swimsuit she was wearing a loose, flowing cover-up in a brilliant blue, purple, and green pattern, with these pompom things around the edges. She looked a bit like a peacock who'd had a run-in with my grandma's knitting basket. It was kind of a lot, but she pulled it off.

"You made that?! Coooool," I said, genuinely impressed. Even Beamer murmured a sound that was something like approval.

Leila grinned and kept talking, spilling out her whole life story in rapid succession. Here's the gist: her parents moved here from Lebanon before she was born; she has two older brothers who are completely useless; she turns eighteen in four months; she has a crush on a guy named Alex at her school; when she's not in her room working on her designs, she likes to read romance novels and hang out with her friends (who had mostly abandoned her today to work in their various retail/hospitality jobs in town, which was why she had been available to "adopt" us—her words); she broke her arm one time when she was seven; she's petrified of flying but loves driving. I could go on (she did) but that would defeat the purpose of the "gist."

And honestly? By the time she was done, I think I was a little bit in love with her. I think Beamer was too. She was loud and warm and bright, like the sun.

A shadow fell over us as we lay there chatting, and I looked up to see Sebastian and Anna. In all the talk I'd almost forgotten about them. (But not quite.)

"You're on my towel," Anna said to Leila.

Leila jumped up. "Oh, sorry, I promise I didn't get it wet," she said, laughing. By that stage, I'd noticed she ended a lot of her sentences with a laugh.

Anna wasn't laughing. She looked Leila up and down as we introduced them.

"Do you love it? I made it myself," Leila said, calling out Anna's blatant stare at her outfit.

"Isn't it gorgeous?" I added.

"Maybe you should get her to make you one, Maisie," Anna replied. "Then you won't have to wear those ratty old board shorts."

Everyone was silent for a second.

Then Beamer said, "Oi, make me one too. I reckon it'd look really nice with *my* ratty old board shorts."

Leila laughed. "I'd love to make you guys something! Come over to my place, I'll take your measurements!"

"Oh, no," I said. "I mean, thank you. But it's fine."

"No, I'm fully serious! This is what I live for. You'd be doing me a favor."

"Go on, Maisie. Do your new friend a favor," Anna said. She was lying down on her towel now, and Sebastian spread out on the other side of her.

"Here, give me your phone, I'll put in my deets," Leila said.

I handed my mobile to her, and Beamer quietly passed his over too. She headed off soon after that, but she insisted we hang out again, adding me and Beamer on multiple social networks before she left.

We walked into town for lunch and then returned to the beach. I'd suggested we go back to the cabin and watch a movie instead, but Beamer was the only one who was keen on that and I did *not* want to be stuck alone with him all afternoon.

Instead, I sat there on the beach as the others alternated between cooling down in the water and cooking in the sun. At one point, when they were all heading into the water *again*, Sebastian said to me, "You coming, Maise?" and I said, "Nah."

Which felt like progress compared to my usual squeaks.

It's a shame it paled in comparison to all the progress Anna was making. *She* had no problems chatting to "Seb," as she'd already taken to calling him. She laughed loudly and enthusiastically at all his jokes and even asked him to teach her how to surf. He happily obliged.

The thing is…Sebastian doesn't know how to surf. I mean, he's really athletic and all, but he never quite got the hang of hanging ten. He did try to learn when we were younger, but after one spectacularly bad attempt landed him in hospital with a mild concussion, he decided to stick to boogie boarding and body surfing, much to his mum's relief.

He miraculously seemed to have forgotten all about that little trauma today, though. Not to mention the minor details of

a) not knowing how to surf, and

b) not even owning a surfboard.

When Beamer said to him, "Mate, what do you know about surfing?" Sebastian just shot him a look and said, "I know enough."

Off he and Anna went down to the wet sand. Turns out they didn't need surfboards for this lesson. They didn't even need to go in the water. All they had to do was lie in the sand while Sebastian showed Anna—with his hands, of course—which body parts she had to move. When it came to her going from lying to crouching to standing, Sebastian had to get right behind her and guide her through it. There was a lot of giggling involved.

I'm pretty sure if Anna actually tried surfing after that lesson, she'd wind up in hospital with a concussion herself.

Sitting there, stuck with Beamer after all, I quietly burned. And it wasn't because of the sun.

* * *

Okay, I feel bad for being so resentful earlier. I was just braiding Anna's hair, and she said to me, "You know, Maise, I get why you're so obsessed with Seb now. He is pretty great."

"Yeah. Great!" is what I said. "Oh. Shit!" is what I felt.

Then she said, "You get kinda weird around him, though. Really quiet. You've got to step up your game. I mean, sure, you've known him since you were kids, but you need to let him know you *now*, you know? He needs to see how special you are. Then he won't be able to help but fall in love with you."

See? I should stop being so selfish. Anna vowed to help me as my designated wingwoman, drawing me into conversations with Sebastian and hopefully alleviating the whole squeaking situation.

"If all else fails, just ask him questions about himself. Guys love that," she said.

"But like...I already know everything there is to know about Sebastian. What the hell would I ask about?"

"You can't know *everything*. It's worth a try, hey?"

"I guess..."

"And Maise, we've got to do something about your beachwear. Today's look was not hot."

I groaned. "There is no look on me that is *not* not hot."

"Are you kidding? Look how big your boobs are! You need to get the girls out. I'm so jealous. I wish I had boobs like that instead of these pancakes."

"Yeah, too bad the rest of me is just as big."

"Stop it. You're not fat. You're gorgeous."

Even though I knew there was no truth behind Anna's words, it made me feel a bit better knowing that she loved me enough to say them. But there was still no way in hell I was getting my boobs or anything else out on the beach.

"I have nothing to wear," I said.

"Why don't we go shopping first thing in the morning? I saw heaps of surf shops in town when we got lunch today. They've got to have something."

"I don't know..." If there are seven layers of hell, then swimwear shopping is the very last of them—i.e. the absolute pits (jeans shopping and bra shopping follow closely behind in layers five and six).

But Anna looked at me with such a hopeful, pleading expression. I thought that with her support, maybe it wouldn't be so bad. Then I thought, wait, I'm supposed to be acting *less* selfish.

"Hang on a minute, I thought this trip was about making *you* feel better, not me," I said.

"Making you feel better will make me feel better," Anna replied. And we hugged, and I felt so grateful to have her as a friend, and that's how I ended up agreeing to go bikini shopping tomorrow morning followed by another day at the beach with Sebastian Lee.

Which pretty much brings you up to date on Everything That Has Happened Since Yesterday. Aaaand I've stayed up way too late writing all this down. At least you're looking *considerably* less empty than you were a couple of hours ago, DJ.

Won't Mum be impressed!

Monday, 18 December

3 things I discovered today:

1. I have to admit, writing things down actually feels kinda good.

Evidence: Last night's epic vent session in this here journal lifted some of the weight off my shoulders (not literally, ugh). Just don't tell Mum or Ms. Singh, okay?

2. Keep your expectations low. That way you won't get disappointed.

Evidence: *Dirty Dancing*/life.

3. The phrase "sweating like a pig" has nothing to do with pigs, but is in fact a reference to pig iron and its production process.

Evidence: Some article I found when I googled "sweating like a pig" while I was lying on the beach... sweating like a pig.

* * *

Oh, DJ, what a day. It started out bad, and it ended up worse.

Let's start with the bad, shall we? Don't worry, we'll get to the worse stuff in time.

BIKINI SHOPPING.

Sadly, real life is not like the movies. There was no montage of Anna and me trying on various outfits, pulling faces, dancing around and having a glorious time, while a track like "Girls Just Wanna Have Fun" played over the top. There was no "stick you" moment to snobby salespeople, no triumphant moment of glory when I found the perfect bikini. There was definitely no finding a magical item of clothing that somehow fit both me and Anna and would take us on adventures we've never even dreamed of.

Here's what there was:

Anna: "We're looking for an amazing swimsuit for my amazing friend."

Salesperson: "What's your size?"

Me: *mumbles incoherently*

Salesperson: "We have this piece and this piece available in that size."

Anna: "That's it?"

Me: *dying*

Anna: "Come on, Maisie, let's try that place down the road."

End scene. Repeat four times over, with only slight variations, such as:

Salesperson: "Sorry, we don't carry that size."

OR

Salesperson: "You could try these separates? They look great together!" (When they didn't match at all.)

Finally, we reached a shop that had absolutely gorgeous swimsuit AND the salesperson said they carried my size. I almost felt hopeful. Almost. Then I saw the price tags. A top alone cost at least $150 and a one-piece was over $200.

"Come on, let's get out of here," I said, and walked out.

"What are you doing? They have some really nice things," Anna said as she followed after me.

"Did you see the prices?! I told you this would be impossible."

Anna bit her lip. "Hey, I think there's one more store we haven't tri—"

"Anna, I love you, but come on. It's time to give up."

"No! The perfect swimsuit could be waiting for you in there. You won't know unless you at least take a look."

She grabbed my hand and practically dragged me to the last store. I was in there for all of three seconds before I froze, staring up at two huge posters behind the counter.

Anna looked up to see what had caught my attention. "Oh my god, is that your sister?"

Yep. There was Eva, on stage, in a blue-sequined bikini and high, high heels, her tanned and toned body posed, poised, and perfect—the words "this could be you" scrawled over her flat stomach. And there was Eva again, this time in a pink strapless evening dress, a grin on her face, tears in her eyes, and a tiara on her head, with the words "Enter Now!" over her perky (thanks to the chicken fillets I knew were stuffed inside her bra) cleavage.

I spun around, walked straight out of the store, and kept walking down the road.

"Maisie, wait! What was that?" Anna said, chasing after me.

"It's this ridiculous pageant they do here every year: *Cobbers Bay Miss Teen Queen*," I said, affecting an announcer voice. "Eva won when she was sixteen. Guess she's part of the advertising now."

Anna was quiet. She knows Eva and I don't get on, although she doesn't know the full details of why. I've always been too embarrassed to tell her—to tell anyone.

Then she said, "Who cares about Eva! Why don't we go back and actually look in that shop? You never know—"

"I do know. It's not going to happen."

"You're so stubborn sometimes."

I stuck my tongue out at her, and she stuck out hers back.

"Seriously, let's just go to the beach," I said.

"Okay, but...what are you going to wear?"

I let out a fake-sob-that-almost-wasn't-fake.

"Look, why don't you show me the swimsuits you have?" Anna said gently. "They can't be that bad. They've gotta be better than those board shorts you were wearing, honestly."

We went back to the cabin, and I put on my swimsuit. The expression on Anna's face said, *I'm trying to keep a straight face and, oh god, how do I say this nicely,* but all her mouth said was, "Ummm..."

"It's alright," I said. "Let's just go." I put my jeans and t-shirt back on over the top of my swimsuit, and didn't take them off all day.

Not when I was sweating like pig iron on the beach, while everyone else went in the water.

Not when Sebastian said to me for the second time, "You coming, Maise?" and I said, "Nah," and *then* he said, "C'mon, aren't you boiling?" and I said, "Nah," while trying to subtly wipe the sweat off my upper lip with my equally sweaty arm.

And definitely not when Beamer decided to intermittently run from the water up to where I was sitting and *shake himself off above me like a goddamn dog*, saying, "Come on, Maisie Martin, the water's beautiful," before running back in.

DJ, at this point, you're probably wondering if Anna's plan to talk me up and draw me into conversation with Sebastian Lee was more successful than her plan to get me into a hot new bikini. Well, I hope you don't mind spoilers (personally, I'm torn on them: sometimes they can enhance my enjoyment, and other times they make me really, really mad), because here is a big one: IT WASN'T.

Oh, she asked him lots of questions and tried to include me, but I was still struggling to move past monosyllabic responses like "nah," "yeah," "ha," "uhhh," and "mmmm." At one point Beamer quietly said to me, "Are you on LinkedIn, Maisie Martin? 'Cos I'd like to endorse you for your conversational skills."

"Is anyone even on LinkedIn? What are you, a forty nine-year-old investment banker?" I hissed at him.

"Whoa, whoa, whoa, don't sprain your tongue there. That was a lot of words in one go."

In response, I stuck out said tongue. Beamer grinned.

Which really made me want to show him. I turned to Sebastian.

"So, Seb—Sebastian," I managed to get out. Then my mind went blank. *Think of something, Maisie. Think.* Sebastian was looking at me expectantly. "Uhhhh..."

I heard Beamer chuckling behind me.

"How's school going?" I finally squeaked.

Sebastian made a face. "Ugh, I don't even want to think about it."

"Oh." I glanced over at Anna, who gave me a tight smile.

Sebastian sighed. "I'm so done with it. And Mum won't get off my back. She's all, 'I know you've got a brain in that head, Sebastian, why aren't you using it?!'"

"She sounds like my mum," Anna said.

"Really?" Sebastian tilted his head her way, a smile on his face. "My condolences."

"Hey, your mum's not that bad," Beamer said to him.

Sebastian scoffed. "Yeah right. She won't even let me go to Penang with Dad and the twins in February.

She reckons I can't afford to miss any school, especially with the marks I'm getting."

Sebastian's family makes the trip to Malaysia every few years, and I know how much he loves going over there. He's really close to his cousins, despite the distance. I was working up the courage to say something about this when Beamer broke in with, "Ah, don't worry, Sebby. I told ya, I'll tutor you. Have you up to scratch in no time."

I snorted at the idea that Beamer could teach Sebastian anything.

"I had to get a tutor last year," Anna said. "Mainly for math. It's sooooo painful."

"Right?!" Sebastian said. "It's like, when are we ever going to use this shit after school?"

"Totally!" Anna said. The two of them shared a smile. "Maisie's brilliant at math, though, aren't you Maise?" Anna added, looking at me pointedly. "And English. She's so smart."

I laughed nervously. After a moment, I said to Sebastian, "I, um, I bet you kill it at English."

He scrunched up his nose. "Nah. That's even worse than math. All Shakespeare and poetry. Bo-*ring*. No offense if you're into that. It just does my head in."

"But—" I was about to protest, thinking about Sebastian's own poetry, and then I realized he was probably saying those things because he didn't want anyone to know about it. I swallowed the rest of my sentence.

"But what?" Sebastian prompted.

"Oh. Um. Nothing."

"Okay," he said, that bemused (or whatever the word for it is) expression appearing on his face.

Yep. I was totally nailing this whole conversation thing.

"Seen any good movies lately?" Anna said in a loud voice. A sure sign the situation was desperate.

"We saw the new *Star Wars* last week," Sebastian said. "It was amazing. The last five minutes..."

He trailed off and Beamer started laughing.

"Oh god, did you cry?" Anna said with a giggle.

"Sobbed like a baby," Beamer said.

"Hey, you did too," Sebastian shot back.

"I was talking about myself."

"Don't worry, so did Maisie," Anna said, smiling at me encouragingly. I felt a surge of gratitude. This was my SHIT. Plus there was history there with me and Sebastian. It was perfect—I just needed to come up with a witty remark to encapsulate all of that. I was still putting my thoughts together when Anna continued, filling the conversational gap I was leaving wide open.

"Honestly, I don't get it," she said. "The movie was kind of a snoozefest. And who cares if—"

"Blasphemy!" Beamer interrupted.

"No way!" Sebastian said.

"Ughhhh..." I gurgled. God, I was getting worse.

"Have you seen the originals?" Sebastian asked Anna.

"Noooooo. Maisie tried to get me to watch them, but we got halfway through the first one and I begged her to release me. Hey, Maise?"

"Yeah," I managed.

Then Sebastian said, "Maise, remember when we used to watch them all the time?"

I had to remind myself to breathe.

"I swear, our mums would put them on every night just to get us to sit still for longer than five minutes. But then we'd be up and playing along anyway," he added with a smile.

"Let me guess: you were Han Solo," Beamer said to Sebastian. He turned to me. "And you were Princess Leia."

"Nah—Chewbacca," I said, as nonchalantly as I could. Everyone laughed, including Anna, because even she knew who that was.

"Why the hell would you be that big furry thing when you could be a princess?" she asked.

"Hey, Chewie was the best!" Sebastian said, grinning at me. "You can't have Han without Chewie. And Maisie can do *brilliant* Wookiee noises."

I returned his smile. His words were finally making me start to relax, and even feel a bit warm inside.

"Go on, let's hear 'em then," said Beamer.

"Go on, Maise," said Sebastian.

Which is how I wound up sitting on the beach, in front of my best friend, the boy I'm in love with, and Beamer, making WOOKIEE NOISES. 'Cos nothing screams sexy like WOOKIEE NOISES.

(Okay, look, they probably scream sexy to some people, no judgment, but *oh god*, not coming from me, not in front of these people.)

I knew I'd made a mistake when, while Sebastian and Beamer were laughing and trying to make the noises themselves, Anna was subtly doing a "cut it out" gesture with her hand below her chin.

Uh-oh. I had to get back on track. I swallowed, took a deep breath, and said, "Hey, remember that time we tried to make rootleaf stew, like Yoda eats?"

Which made Sebastian grin again. Phew. Maybe I could do this after all.

"Aw, yeah, it was disgusting!" he said. "We put bark and leaves and mud and god knows what else in hot water and actually tried to eat it."

We were all laughing again. Feeling quite proud of myself, I said, "It was so gross! I swear I got actual worms from it."

Which made Sebastian and Beamer laugh more, while Anna widened her eyes and mouthed *What?!* at me.

Maybe I could *not* do this after all.

"Hey, speaking of movies," Anna said, pulling out that trusty old segue even though we weren't strictly speaking about movies anymore, "I saw a poster for some kind of outdoor cinema thing in town this morning. It sounds really fun."

"Oh, yeah, Beachside Cinema," Sebastian said. "It's pretty cool. They set up a big screen in the park down by the main beach."

"Oooh, awesome."

"Hey, why don't we go tonight?"

"Great idea, Seb." Anna smiled at him and glanced over at me. "Sounds perfect."

It did sound perfect. So perfect, in fact, it was something I'd actually fantasized about doing with Sebastian on multiple occasions (sure, we *had* been together a couple of times—but somehow with both of our families in tow it wasn't quite the same).

I mentioned as much to Anna as I was doing her makeup later. I'm really good at makeup, thanks to countless hours sucked into YouTube beauty tutorial wormholes. I hardly ever wear it—usually I just play around with it at home—but tonight Anna suggested we both go all-out.

"I knew it," she said with a smile.

"I never told you, though. How did you know?"

"Because I know you, Maise."

By the time I was finished doing our makeup, I was pretty excited, despite the horrors of the morning and the errors of the afternoon. Anna looked absolutely stunning, and I wasn't feeling so bad myself.

When we met up with the guys to walk over to Beachside Cinema, we apparently made a pretty good impression. Sebastian Lee let out a small "wow," and handed me and Anna a flower each. I practically swooned on the spot. I could tell he'd picked them from the bushes near the beach path, but it was the sweetest gesture. Even Beamer didn't ruin my mood when he whistled and said, "Don't youse scrub up alright?"

I said, "Ew, don't use 'youse.'" But I couldn't stop grinning. The night was off to a very good start.

Then I saw what was playing at Beachside Cinema.

"*Dirty Dancing*?!" Suddenly my dream evening was turning into a nightmare.

"I've never seen it," Anna said.

"That worked out well, then," Sebastian said with a smile. The two of them stepped forward to buy us all tickets with the money our mums had forked over.

"Awwww, why are you pouting, Maisie Martin?" Beamer said with mock sympathy. "Isn't this, like, one of your favorite movies?"

"I hate this movie, actually."

"What? I thought you were obsessed with it. You and your sister—"

"That was a long time ago. I know it's hard for you to believe, but some people mature after the age of twelve."

"Look, this isn't exactly my favorite movie, either. Should we bail?" He held out his hand as though I might actually take it.

Sebastian appeared and put a ticket in Beamer's outstretched hand, then offered one to me.

"Hey, Maise, I just saw your sister," he said, gesturing in the direction of the ticket booth.

I swear my heart skipped like ten beats. I was not mentally prepared to see her for at least a few more days. "What? Where?!"

And then I saw it. Another one of those *Miss Teen Queen* posters. Beamer saw it at the same time as me.

"Hey, I remember that. We all went to watch," he said.

"Yeah. It was the longest day," Sebastian said.

"Swimsuit competition was alright though," Beamer countered, waggling his eyebrows.

"You're so gross," I said, for about the seven hundredth time in our lives.

He laughed and glanced back at the poster, lingering over Eva's cleavage, no doubt. "Jeez, did she really win a thousand bucks?"

"Nah, that's the prize if you win nationals," I said. "She came third."

Anna snorted. "Bet she *loved* that."

I laughed. Then Sebastian said, "Bet you'd win it," and for a second I couldn't breathe. Until I realized he was talking to Anna. He'd nudged her with his arm and smiled. She let out a high-pitched giggle and said, "No, I wouldn't." And he said, "Yeah, you would," and she said, "No, I wouldn't," and they kept going back and forth like that until finally I said, "I bet *I* would."

That shut them both up. After a second Sebastian said, "Yeah, you'd totally own the talent competition with that Wookiee impression." He winked at me, and my heart grew two sizes. He started walking toward our designated beanbags (yes, beanbags), still talking to me. I fell into step beside him.

"Looks like you're finally getting me to watch this movie, eh?" he said.

"I can't believe you remember that."

"Remember what?" Anna asked from behind us.

"Maisie tried to make me watch this when we were younger. I think we got about five minutes in, and I refused to watch any more," Sebastian said, smiling. "I promise I'll sit all the way through it this time."

"Huh. Guess some people really do mature after the age of twelve," Beamer said.

I shot him a look, and he responded with a smirk.

"Thirty-four, that's me," Sebastian said as we reached our beanbags. He did a little twist-jump in the air before crash-landing on one of the middle beanbags in our little row of four. I looked at my ticket. Thirty-three. Oh god. Right next to him. I gulped and tried to sit down as gracefully as I could (hint: not very). Anna grinned at me as she took her seat (very gracefully) on Sebastian's other side. Aaaand Beamer dropped down on *my* other side.

I wasn't sure how I felt about the situation—mainly because I was feeling a lot of things. Grateful (to Anna), nervous (to be so close to Sebastian), excited (Sebastian again), hopeful (Sebastian), annoyed (Beamer, of course), terrified (of the movie and its potential to open up old wounds).

Then the movie started, and it was weird. But in a good kinda way. Like, how is it that even when you haven't seen a movie in years, just watching the opening credits can stir some long-dormant part of your soul? I'd avoided watching it for so long because I thought it'd make me feel angry and upset, but instead it just felt like...coming home.

I know, I know, I'm talking about *Dirty Dancing* here, it's not like it's *Citizen* freaking *Kane*.

But this movie, despite everything...it's a part of me. I felt content. And a little bit emotional. I managed to make it to the bit where Baby confronts her father about how he let her down (*"There are a lot of things about me that aren't what you thought, but if you love me, you have to love all the things about me."*), before feeling like I might cry.

That's when I looked over at Anna. Her eyes were glued to the screen. And, between us, so were Sebastian's. Sebastian's hand, however...was resting on Anna's thigh. And his thumb was drawing little tiny circles on her skin. And that's when I noticed they both had smiles on their faces. And that's when I felt like I really would cry.

"I'm going to get popcorn," I squeaked before hauling myself up as quickly as I could (hint: not very. Have you ever tried to get out of a beanbag? Of course you haven't, DJ, you're an inanimate object. Well, let me tell you, it's not easy. Forget looking graceful—I was about half a step away from falling flat on my face). I finally managed it and rushed away, but when I reached the food truck at the back of the park I didn't join the line. Instead, I stood staring at the menu board without really seeing what was on it. I was too busy trying to stop the tears from falling. It made my throat burn.

I felt a gentle hand on my shoulder and spun around, relieved.

"Anna, I—"

Only it wasn't Anna.

And in case you're hoping for a nice romantic moment, sorry. This is real life, remember? Not a movie. So no, it wasn't Sebastian Lee, either.

It was bloody Beamer.

That finally tipped those tears over the edge. I was not in the mood for his shit-stirring. I shook my head, wanting to shake the tears away, shake him away, shake everything away. I turned and ran to a nearby tree, sliding down to sit below it. Beamer followed and sat down next to me.

"Can you just go away, please?" I swabbed at my eyes with the edge of my cardigan sleeve.

He didn't say a word, but he didn't go away either. He silently reached into his pocket, pulled out a neatly folded hanky and held it out to me.

I screwed up my nose.

"It's clean, I swear," he said.

I took it from him, feeling really weird about literally everything that was happening, and mumbled "thanks." I wiped my eyes and dabbed at my nose before trying to give it back, but it was his turn to screw up his nose.

"Hold on to it for now, eh?"

I suddenly felt really embarrassed. Not that I cared all that much what Beamer thought of me—but what would he tell Sebastian?

"Beamer—"

And then, because he's Beamer, and because this is my life, he farted. FARTED. It was a really loud and obnoxious one too. It was so unexpected (although I don't know why, this was Beamer, after all), I just stared at him for a moment.

Then I woke up and gave him a whack on the shoulder. "God, Beamer, you're so disgusting!"

He laughed.

"Why are you so disgusting?!" I gave him another whack.

That just made him laugh more.

"It's not funny! It's gross!" I grabbed his shoulder and shook him gently, but by that stage I couldn't help it—I was laughing too.

That's when he got quiet and said, "You alright, Maisie Martin?"

"I was fine before you came." I gave him a shove.

"Yeah, nah, it's just...d'you-maybe-wanna-talk-about-it?" Beamer has this way of speaking, like he can't be bothered to open his mouth very far, and the words have to force themselves through his lips so that they either come out really slow and dragged out, or they all tumble through in a rush and get smashed together.

"If I did, do you think it would be with you?"

He scratched the back of his head. "Nah, yeah, but uh...you could, y'know. F'you wanted to." Those words sounded extra painful to let out.

I sighed, twisting his hanky in my hands. "Beamer, not to sound ungrateful, but who carries a *hanky* around these days?!" (Yes, DJ, I will accept points for that smooth subject change, thank-you-very-much.)

Beamer smiled. "Hey, us forty-nine-year-old investment bankers always come prepared."

I rolled my eyes and looked at it again. "Wait a sec ...does this have your *initials* embroidered on it?!" The letters E. I. B. were sewn into the corner in dark blue stitching.

He let out one of those huffs that's almost a laugh, but not quite. "Uh, yeah. My gran does that to all of 'em. Every birthday and Christmas, she gives me a whole new batch. It's tradition. A nice reminder that...that someone loves me." He looked away.

"Oh..." I didn't know what to say to that. Then I realized that his token of love was now covered in not just my snot and tears, but also my makeup.

"Oh my god, Beamer, I'm sorry. I've ruined it."

He looked at it and smiled. "Nah, s'alright. It'll wash out. Besides, I've got another two hundred of 'em! You've ruined your makeup though."

I pulled my phone out of the back pocket of my jeans and opened the selfie camera to inspect the damage on my face. He was right—it was a mess. I licked a corner of the hanky and attempted to fix it.

I heard Beamer draw in breath to speak, and I thought he was going to comment on how gross the spit-clean was. Instead he said, very softly, "You like him, don't you?"

"What?! Who?!" I glanced at him and he just raised his eyebrows.

"That's why you're upset, right? You've had it bad for Sebby for years and here he is, putting the moves on your best mate."

"No! Shut up!" The emotion in my voice betrayed me. I waited for him to start hurling jokes or insults, but instead he surprised me again by saying, "It's alright. I get it."

"You get what?"

"Sebby is pretty dreeeaamy," he said, smirking and fluttering his eyelashes. And there was the joke.

"Yeah, but...I mean, I've hardly spoken to him in years. Not exactly a sign of love, is it?" I was getting desperate.

"Mmmm, or that's exactly what it is."

"Oh, and you know so much, don't you?"

He shrugged. Picked up a stick and started absent-mindedly drawing a pattern in the dirt.

I groaned. "Does Sebastian know?"

He shrugged again. "Never spoken about it."

"Great, I don't even rate a mention."

Beamer didn't say anything.

"You know what's funny?" I said, annoyed now. "We used to be really close. We played together all the time when we were kids."

"Yeah, *Star Wars*. I heard." He dropped the stick and looked at me. "So what happened?"

"You showed up." I poked him and he snorted. "Honestly? I guess...yeah, I started to like him." There was no hiding from the truth, apparently. "I mean, I always thought he was cute—" here Beamer snorted again "—but one day I..."

"One day you...?" Beamer prompted me to finish.

Fuck it, I thought. I'd come this far.

"Um, have you ever read Sebastian's poetry?"

"Sebastian's *poetry*?" The way he said it made it sound like those words didn't go together, like I'd said "the Pope's wife" or "Disney's pornography."

"Ugh, forget it. Forget I said anything, okay?"

"Nah, nah, tell me."

I sighed. Might as well keep digging.

"Alright, but you have to swear you won't tell Sebastian or *anyone*. Promise me!"

He held up his pinkie finger, and I linked mine with his. He bent his head over our joined hands and kissed his own thumb. I did the same to mine, feeling a little ridiculous.

"There," he said. "That's an unbreakable bond, Maisie Martin."

I unlinked my hand from his and started twisting his hanky between my fingers again.

He leaned back and said, "So?"

"You're going to think it's silly."

He didn't say anything, just sat there with an *I'm waiting* look on his face. I sighed again.

"Look, I'm guessing he'd hate for you to know this since he's never told you himself, but Sebastian... Sebastian writes the most beautiful poetry. When I read it, I realized there was so much more to him than I thought. Like, he's got all this stuff bubbling below the surface that maybe he can't say out loud, but he can *write* it and create something wonderful, you know? There was this one poem that was all about colors, but really it was about loneliness, and I had no idea he felt that way, and I've never read anything that got to me like that and I think—" here I noticed a smirk growing on Beamer's face "—oh god, you promised you wouldn't tell him. Please don't say anything, *please please please*."

He tried to straighten his face. I could tell it was a struggle. Finally, slowly and deliberately, he said, "Seb...let you read his poetry?"

Shit.

"Ummmmm...I guess *let* would probably be the wrong word."

He raised an eyebrow.

Fuck. "I, um, I...kinda snuck a peek one day when I saw his journal open on his bed and no one was around, okay? Please don't say anything, Beamer— you promised!"

He laughed. "Hoo-hoo-hoo, aren't you the sly one, eh?" He nudged me with his elbow.

I felt sick.

"Looking all sweet and innocent and then snooping in other people's bedrooms and reading their secret thoughts. Didn't know you had it in you, Maisie Martin."

I groaned. "You're not going to tell him, are you?"

"Ah, don't worry about it. I pinkie-promised, remember? I'll never breathe a word of it to Sebby." He grinned wickedly. "Didn't promise I'd never mention it to you again, though."

"Oh god, what have I done?"

He chuckled. "So, uh...you really liked his poetry, hey?"

I let out a frustrated noise and threw the now-balled-up hanky at his head. It was a completely ineffectual missile, fluttering to the ground between us.

Now he was really laughing. Me and my pathetic feelings were just so amusing to him. I was contemplating whether murdering him would be justifiable homicide (pretty sure any jury would be on my side), and must have been shooting one of my best death stares, because he paused and said, "Alright, alright, chill, Maisie Martin. Your secret is safe with me, okay?"

I looked at him dubiously.

He rubbed his thumb over his lips, thoughtful. "Would it make you feel better to know my secret?"

I narrowed my eyes. "Depends on what it is."

He exhaled. "Okay, we've confirmed that you like Seb, a fact that's been pretty obvious for years."

"Yep, literally happened two minutes ago, no need for the recap, thanks."

"Well, there's someone that I like, which I think is pretty obvious too. Any guesses?" He had a suggestive half-smile on his face. Although I'd never really considered it before, it didn't take me long to figure out. The Venn diagram of people we both know is pretty small, and the people within crush-worthy age range even smaller (not that I'd put it past Beamer to be a creep about one of our mums, to be honest).

"It's not Anna, is it?"

His look said *as if,* although I don't know what would be so *as if* about it. But that left only one option.

"Ugh, so you like Eva. Get in line. You know she's dating a girl now, right?"

"Maisie—"

"Sorry if you had big dreams of sweeping her off her feet. But even if she were single, even if she were into guys, I doubt she'd give you a second glance."

He swallowed hard. "Right. Got it. Thanks." He looked annoyed.

I felt a bit bad then, but I didn't know what to say. I reached down to pick up his hanky, and the initials caught my eye again.

"Hey, what *is* your first name, anyway?"

He didn't say anything for a moment, but then relented. "What, one secret out of me isn't enough for tonight?"

"Why is it a secret?"

No answer.

"Come oooonnnnn, tell me!"

"You know, Maisie Martin, I'd tell you, but then I'd have to kill you."

"Ah, the most overused line in cinematic history."

"Nah, c'mon, that's gotta be: 'We can do this the easy way, or the hard way,'" he said, putting on a gravelly action hero-style voice.

"Or, 'We've got company!'" I said, imitating his tone.

"'You just don't get it, do you?'"

"'It's not what it looks like!'"

"'We're not so different, you and I.'"

"'Is that all you've got?'"

"'*Danger* is my middle name.'"

"Hey, what *is* your middle name?"

"It's—ha, nice try, Maisie Martin. You nearly got me there."

We both laughed.

"Come on," Beamer said, getting up and dusting off his butt. "You don't want to miss the big finish."

My gut twisted as I remembered why I'd walked away in the first place. But I was feeling a bit calmer now. What I really wanted to do was talk to Anna. So when Beamer reached down to help me up, I took his hand.

"Don't think this means we're friends now," I said to his back as he led me to our seats.

"Ha! Definitely not, Maisie Mart—hey, we never got that popcorn," he said, suddenly spinning around and trying to push me back toward the food truck. "Come on, we better get there before it closes. Mush!"

"Beamer, wha—" And that's when I saw it, over his shoulder.

Sebastian Lee. *My* Sebastian Lee. Leaning over. And kissing Anna.

I opened my mouth in shock, and Beamer shuffled so he was blocking them from my line of sight. He had a guilty look on his face.

"What is this? You keep me occupied so Sebastian can get lucky?!"

"What? Maisie, no—"

"I've seen this move before, Beamer. The wingman distracts the fuggo so his mate can score the hottie. How *generous* of you. I should have known." I spun around and ran off, this time going straight past the food truck, straight past that damn tree, and through the gate. I heard Beamer calling after me, but I didn't stop. Not until I was back in the cabin, in my bedroom, having rushed past Mum and Laura on the veranda, and I closed the door behind me with a thud.

I heard Mum knock. "Maisie? Maisie, are you alright? What's going on? Why are you home already?"

"I'm just not feeling well. I'm alright!"

She slid the door open a bit and stuck her head in. "Where's Anna? Didn't she come home with you?"

"No, I told her not to worry about it. I think I just need to rest." Mum walked over and put her hand on my forehead. I swatted it away. "Mum, I'm fine, I just need some sleep."

"I'm not very impressed that Anna would—"

"Mum!"

She sighed. "Alright. I'll just be in here if you need anything, okay?"

"Okay."

She slid the door shut, but five minutes later she was back. She didn't say anything, just put some aspirin and a glass of water down next to my bed and walked out again, closing the door behind her.

I tried to call Dad a couple of times, but it just went through to voicemail, which was weird. He normally picks up straight away, no matter what he's doing, unless he's watching a movie. Maybe that was it. I didn't bother leaving him a message, because I didn't know what to say. I just wanted to hear his voice.

I don't know how much later it was when Anna walked in, but it felt like ages.

"Maise, are you okay? You and Beamer both disappeared, and I was like, 'oh my god, has he kidnapped her?' But your mum said you were sick?"

She walked over to the bed and kneeled down next to me, a worried look on her face. The image of Sebastian kissing her flashed before my eyes.

"Yeah," I said. "I feel really sick."

"You should have let me know. I would have come back with you."

"I didn't want to interrupt your fun," I said, a bite slipping into my tone.

"Maise..."

I rolled over to face the wall. "Forget it, Anna. I just need some sleep. Can you turn off the light?"

"Sure," she said quietly, flipping off the switch and slipping out of the room. Through the wall, I heard her in the bathroom, no doubt going through the many stages of her rigorous night-time skincare routine. After several minutes, she returned.

"Maise—" she started to say, and I made a loud snoring noise. She sighed and climbed into the bunk above me. I let out a few more snores for good measure. After a while, I heard Anna snoring for real, while I lay awake, staring at the space where she was sleeping above me.

Tuesday, 19 December

2 things I discovered today:

1. Apparently there is such a thing as morning people. They're not a myth.

Evidence: I didn't get much sleep last night. By 5:30 AM I couldn't take it anymore and crept out to go for a walk along the beach. There were actually a lot of people out and about, and, worst of all, they seemed HAPPY about it. They were all "good morning!" and "beautiful day, isn't it?" like they wouldn't rather be in bed asleep if they could help it. (To be honest, the sunrise *was* pretty spectacular. But you know what else is? Sleep.)

2. I think I have a new friend.

Evidence: Leila Khouri. She's kind of the best.

* * *

I knew Mum and Anna had woken up when the messages started.

Mum: *MAISIE! WHERE ARE YOU! ARE YOU ALIVE!*

Anna: *Maise? Where are you? Are you OK?*

Mum: *MAISIE MARTIN! ANSWER YOUR PHONE! ARE YOU DEAD!*

Me: *MUM. I just went for a walk. Chill.*

Mum: [. . .]

Mum: *IF A KIDNAPPER IS RECEIVING THESE MESSAGES I WANT YOU TO KNOW I AM CALLING THE POLICE!!!!*

Mum: *NEXT TIME ANSWER YOUR PHONE THE FIRST TIME, MISSY, NOT THE THIRD! I FORGOT TO MENTION WHEN WE WERE CHATTING JUST NOW THAT I'M GOING SHOPPING WITH LAURA! HAVE A GOOD DAY!*

Anna: *?????*

Me: *Hey Anna! Sorry, I woke up early and didn't want to wake you. I just bumped into Leila, remember her? She invited me over. You'll be alright without me this morning, yeah?*

Anna: [. . .]

Anna: [. . .]

Anna: *K.*

Me: *Hey Leila! It's Maisie, remember me? You said we should hang out, and I know you might not have meant it, but just in case...wanna hang out?*

Leila: *Hey gorgeous girl! Of course I remember you. And I totally meant it! I'm working with Mum this morning, come have brekkie and then we can HANG OUT!*

I stared at Anna's *K* for a while. No *O* meant it definitely wasn't *OK* (I mean, quite literally, and also symbolically). But I really wasn't ready to talk about whatever had happened last night, so I tried to push away the tension I felt and headed to Leila's.

Her place is awesome. She lives in a massive house, but it's divided so that the family lives in a private section in the front, and then the back part is a bunch of suites the guests stay in, with a dining room and common room in the center. There's a pool out the back, too, with a big deck and those fancy lounge chairs. I asked Leila if it felt weird to have random strangers in her house all the time, but she said they still have a lot of privacy and she finds meeting new people "inspiring."

After meeting her mum, I can see where she gets her...what is it, confidence? Warmth? *Je ne sais quoi*, as my grandma would say (I just had to google how to spell that fyi).

I felt a bit awkward when I got there, because they

were busy organizing breakfast and I didn't want to get in the way.

"Can I do anything to help?" I said.

"Don't you dare!" Maya (that's Leila's mum) said. She gave me a threatening look, but there was a twinkle in her eyes. "You just sit down here and relax, eat some eggs, and we've got some spare muffins—and, oh, have some of this, and help yourself to a cup of tea or coffee." She handed me a plate piled with food.

"Isn't this for your guests?" I asked.

"You *are* a guest," said Maya.

Leila grinned at me over the fruit platter she was assembling.

"I meant your paying guests."

"Babe," said Leila, "this is a battle you're going to lose, so you may as well quit now. Mama loves feeding people, paying guests or not."

Maya laughed, a big, open laugh like her daughter's. "Exactly. Hush up and eat."

I did as she said, and after a while I began to feel less awkward. Leila and her mum didn't stop chatting as they rushed around. Once they were done, Maya ushered us out of the kitchen, telling us to enjoy the day. Leila led me to her room, and *oh my god*. It was like stepping into a fabric store that had been hit by a tornado and blended together with a

78

dozen Pinterest boards come to life. Her walls were absolutely covered in sketches and photos and things she must have printed out for inspiration, and there were beads and sequins and pompoms and fabric and actual clothes and shoes and handbags all over the place. I could hardly see the bed, let alone the floor. The only clear space in the room was around the sewing machine in the corner.

"Sorry about the mess," Leila said. "I've been working on being tidy. Believe it or not, this is an improvement. It's only taken me seventeen years."

She moved a pile of stuff from a big orange chair and dumped it next to her bed, telling me to take a seat. She shoved more stuff from the bed itself and sat cross-legged on it.

"Where are your friends today?" Leila asked.

"I'm not sure. At the beach, I guess. I haven't seen any of them."

"Did you guys have a fight or something?" She didn't ask it like she was being nosy, but like she actually cared.

"Um, not exactly."

"Is everything okay?"

"Not exactly."

She contemplated me for a moment. "Do you wanna talk about it? I know you haven't known me long, but

I'm a good listener. I swear. And I can keep my mouth shut sometimes." She smiled.

Before I could say anything, a flyer on her floor caught my eye. It was a smaller version of the *Miss Teen Queen* pageant poster, with my sister's smiling face on it.

"What are you doing with that?" I asked.

Leila followed my gaze. "Oh, this? Have you seen the pageant before?" She reached down and picked up the pamphlet.

I nodded. "That's my sister."

"Whhaaaat, are you serious? She's beautiful. I remember when she won a couple of years ago. I hated her dress." Her eyes widened when she realized what she'd said. "Um, I mean, it's just, I go every year to check out the outfits, you know? And most of them are HIDEOUS. And—"

"It's okay," I said with a laugh. "I hated her dress too. It *was* hideous."

Leila smiled, looking relieved.

"Why do you keep going if you think the outfits are hideous?" I asked.

"Oh, well, that's half the fun, isn't it? Mocking them. Also I'm an optimist, and every year I hold out hope that there'll be something decent to look at. I have this dream of seeing some of my designs on that stage...It's silly, I know, but it's honestly the biggest event in this town all year. It'd be the best way to get my stuff noticed. I tried to convince my friend Jo to enter this year so I could dress her, but she just started going on about how it's a patriarchal skeeze-fest, and she wouldn't be caught dead there. I guess she has a point—like, the whole premise is pretty screwed up...but it would be great for my portfolio. Does that make me a terrible person?" She laughed. "It doesn't matter, anyway, because none of my friends would enter."

"Why don't you enter yourself?"

She snorted. "I thought about it, but I couldn't do it. I'm way too shy."

I raised my eyebrows and she laughed.

"What? It's true! Believe me. I'm really shy. I mean, I love talking to people face to face, but get me up on a stage and I freeze up. My Year 7 adviser tried to get me into drama because she said I have a *natural theatricality*—honestly I don't know *what* she could have been talking about, do you? But yeah, every time I tried to say a line in front of a crowd, it just made me want to vom. So I told her I wanted in on the costume department instead and the rest, as they say, is history." She looked at the flyer in her hands again, at Eva's grinning face, and then turned back to me. "Hey, have you ever thought about entering?"

"Me?!"

"You!"

"You're kidding, right?"

"No way! Oh my god, you should do it! And let me dress you! How fun would that be? Please say yes..." She had a huge, hopeful grin on her face.

I thought back to last night, to the moment when I said I could win it. To Sebastian winking at me. And then to him kissing Anna.

I sighed. "There's no point. Look at me."

She looked me up and down. "I'm looking. And?"

"And I'm not exactly beauty pageant material."

"Why the hell not?"

I scrunched up my nose. "Because I'm...I'm a disgusting fat pig who no one wants to see in public, let alone on stage." The words rolled out before I could stop them.

"Whoa. That's a bit harsh," Leila said. She got up from the bed and kneeled in front of me, gently laying a hand on my knee. "And so not true."

I shook my head. "You don't need to do that."

"Do what?"

"Lie to me."

"Babe, I would never. You are not...what was it you said? 'A disgusting fat pig who doesn't belong in public?'" I flinched to hear the words repeated back to me. "That's absurd. You're beautiful. You belong in the world, and on that stage, just as much as *anyone* else."

"Leila, it's okay. I know I'm not beautiful. I'm fat."

"And why can't you be both?" she said with a smile.

I was so shocked, I didn't respond straight away. I'd been expecting her to keep on denying that I was fat, telling me beautiful lies the way Anna did. "You're not fat, you're gorgeous," Anna would say, and I'd be grateful to her for loving me so much that she'd pretend not to see the truth. That's what friends do, right? Not like my mum, who'd say, "Well, you can do something about it, you know," or Eva who...well, anyway, not like Eva. It was a bit of a revelation, what Leila said.

That didn't mean I agreed with it, but she took my silence to mean that I did.

"See? You could be the next Miss Teen Queen!"

"No, I really couldn't. I mean, you have to put your size on the entry form. The judges would take one look at mine and hit delete."

"Hey, can I ask you something?" Leila said. "Putting aside all this stuff about what the judges might think, or anyone else for that matter, do you *want* to enter the pageant? Like, honestly?"

And here's the bit where I admit the truth. You see,

DJ...a small part of me would absolutely love to be in the pageant. To win it.

When we were younger, Eva and I talked about entering together. We couldn't wait until we were both old enough. We'd do a joint talent entry and dance together. We didn't care if that was allowed or not. We'd do it anyway. We had this whole routine we'd choreographed to the music from *Dirty Dancing*, one of the few movies we both adored. And the judges would be so impressed by our talent and beauty they'd hand us both crowns, and we'd be happy, but what would make us happiest wouldn't be winning, it'd be the fact that we did it together.

And then Eva went and did it on her own. And won.

And deep down inside, there's a part of me that wants to do it too.

I confessed as much to Leila. She wasn't lying when she said she's a good listener. She didn't judge me at all or make me feel silly about what I was feeling. And once I started talking, it was like I couldn't have kept the words in even if I tried.

"Okay, how's this sound?" Leila said when I was done. "Why don't we fill out an entry form for you, and if you don't hear anything, it's no loss, right? I mean, same difference as if you hadn't entered anyway. But if they select you to take part, wouldn't that be great? Really, what have you got to lose?"

My last shred of dignity, I thought. But Leila was right. We killed half an hour by filling out the entry form online. And as we went through each question, the idea that my entry would actually see the light of day seemed further and further away. So I just had fun with it, and by the time Leila hit "submit," some of the tightness I'd been carrying around in my chest had uncoiled. Maybe now this whole pageant ridiculousness would be out of my system.

I spent another hour at Leila's, flicking through these vintage magazines from the 1980s and 90s that she collects, doing silly quizzes and laughing at the fashion and slang and "spunks." Then she had to meet up with some friends. She invited me to come along, but I decided to finally face the music. I had to find Anna.

Wednesday, 20 December

2 things I discovered today:

1. It's probably a good idea to face things rather than run away.

Evidence: I actually talked to Anna, and things are better.

2. Junior Mints are bloody delicious.

Evidence: My tastebuds, via the packet I bought at the corner store and ate.

* * *

Alright, DJ, I have a confession: I've been really, really mad at Anna. Surprise! I bet you couldn't tell at all, could you?

I guess I didn't want to say it out loud (or, you know, on paper) because I didn't want to admit it. I didn't want to think about it. I didn't want to face it. Because, well, facing it meant facing the truth: that the person I was most angry at wasn't Anna at all. It wasn't Sebastian Lee, either. It wasn't even Beamer.

It was myself.

I was...I am...angry at myself for so many things.

Like losing my ability to be a functioning person—let alone an attractive one—around Sebastian Lee.

Like holding out any hope he would ever see anything in me anyway.

Like expecting anyone could ever want me when I don't even like looking at myself in the mirror.

Like doing all the things that make me feel bad, despite knowing that they'll make me feel bad.

Like doing all the things that make me feel bad *because* I know that they'll make me feel bad.

Like being caught in a vicious cycle of self-hatred and self-punishment.

Like...

Like...

Like...

Everything.

The thing is, I'm grateful to Anna. She is one of the few people who loves me unconditionally. And who not only loves me, but she actually wants to be around me.

Wanna know how we became friends? (I hope so, because I'm telling you anyway.)

It was the second week of Year 7. I was sitting with my friend Vanessa on the library steps. (Vanessa and I aren't really friends anymore, but that's a whole other story.)

These Year 8 boys were a few steps above us. Out of nowhere, they started pelting us with food. They were laughing as we just sat there in shock. After a minute or two I heard the words, "Fuck off, you knobheads!" and I looked up to see Anna standing in front of me, her hands on her hips, glaring up at those boys. She looked ferocious. And something magical happened. They actually stopped. Anna stuck up her middle finger at them, then looked down at us and said, "C'mon. Come sit with us." She led us across the quad to her group, and I never looked back.

She saved me that day. She's been saving me ever since.

Lately it's been my turn to save her. She's been so broken up about Dan the Dickhead, and she likes to pretend she's fine about her mum ditching her but I know that doesn't help. And yesterday I went AWOL.

I was thinking about all this as I headed back from

Leila's. And my anger began to subside as guilt reared its ugly head.

When I got back to the cabin, no one was around. I began writing everything down from the morning while I waited for someone to show up. If I'm being honest, I was still putting off actually having to talk to Anna.

Finally, I heard laughter on the veranda. I went to the door and there was Anna with Sebastian and Beamer, sitting at the table eating sushi. Beamer spotted me first.

"There you are, Maisie Martin! Where've you been all morning?"

"Around," I said.

"Anna said you weren't feeling great. You okay?" Sebastian asked.

I looked at Anna, who was clearly finding something in her sushi roll fascinating because she was staring intently at it.

"I'm a lot better now, thanks," I said.

Anna looked up at me then, and I tried to smile. She looked really worried.

"Right," she said. "You two, piss off. Maisie and I are going to have some best friend time."

"Alright then, we know when we're not wanted, eh Sebby?" Beamer said, getting up while still shoveling food in his face.

Sebastian stood, briefly resting his hand on Anna's shoulder and saying, "I'll talk to you later."

"See ya," she said.

"Catch ya. Glad you're feeling better, Maise."

They walked away, and then it was just me and Anna. I went over to the table and sat down opposite her. We were quiet for a moment. Then, at the same time, we both said, "I'm sorry."

We laughed, more awkward than amused. I pushed on. "Anna, I'm sorry for disappearing today, I—"

"No, no, don't apologize. I'm the one who's sorry. You...you saw us last night, didn't you?" She swallowed hard. She had a pained expression on her face. "Me and Seb, I mean."

"Yeah. I saw you."

"I'm really sorry, Maisie. I don't know how it happened. He just—I just—he just kissed me, and I was so shocked and—"

"It's okay," I said.

"It's not! It's like rule number one of friendship: don't kiss your best friend's guy. I'm the worst." She looked like she was about to cry.

"That's the thing, though, isn't it?" I said. "He's not my guy. If he was, he wouldn't have kissed you."

"But—"

"It's fine, Anna. I get it."

"It won't happen again, I swear." She looked absolutely miserable.

"Do you want it to happen again?" I asked, sounding way calmer than I felt.

"No! Of course not! I would never want to hurt you like that," she said.

"But you like Sebastian, right?"

Anna bit her lip. Her large, lovely eyes were full of worry. "Maise..."

"Don't worry about it, okay? He's all yours."

"What? No! I would never let a guy come between us." Which was true. Through all the boyfriends she's had (she never stays single for long), Anna has always had time for me and prioritized our friendship. Which was what I was trying to do now.

"He won't," I said. "If he is what you want, if he is going to make you happy, then that's what I want."

Anna was quiet for a moment. "Maisie, I can't," she said. "You've been in love with him for years. It's not going to happen, okay?"

I thought about how much happier she's been over the last few days. About the way I'd seen Sebastian looking at her. The way he had never—would never— look at me. And I told her a beautiful lie, like she'd done for me so many times before.

"Anna, I promise you. It's fine. I'm kind of over him, anyway."

"But—"

I cut her off with a wave of my hand. "Seriously. I think the whole crush thing has been more of a habit than anything else. A way to keep myself entertained. But I've got *you* here now. I don't need a silly crush."

She looked at me carefully, and I leaned forward and rested my chin on my hands, smiling. "Besides," I said. "There's no point in wasting perfectly kiss-able lips." I waggled my eyebrows and she laughed. "I want all the details! Come on!"

She shook her head and changed the subject, telling me about a glitter makeup tutorial she'd seen on You-Tube that she thought I should try. We went inside, dragged out all our makeup, put on some music, and played around until Mum got home with Laura. She took one look at us, laughed, and then pulled out some face masks she'd bought. The four of us spent the rest of the night treating ourselves, and when Lincoln appeared looking for Laura, she told him to go home and tell the others we were in a boy-free zone. Mum even let me and Anna have a bit of wine. It was a total cliché of a girls' night, and you know what? It was really nice. There were some awkward moments—like, whenever Mum mentioned "your father" with a reflexive lip curl, but Laura expertly navigated her away from the topic, for which I was extremely grateful.

And for the first time in days, when I went to bed, I went straight to sleep and slept all night.

* * *

As for today, nothing much to report. Anna and I went for a walk together this morning, then met up with Sebastian and Beamer at the beach. It went about how every other interaction has gone since we got here (Sebastian: his usual friendly self, especially toward Anna; Anna: pretty happy, especially near Sebastian; Beamer: bloody annoying, especially around me; me: quiet and self-conscious—especially around Sebastian and Anna...especially every time I spotted Sebastian's hand on Anna's arm or her thigh or her back. Tracing those tiny little circles and patterns with his fingers...).

"Let's go get some lunch," I said after a while.

"It's way too early. I'm not really hungry yet," Anna protested.

"Yeah, me neither," Sebastian said.

"I'll come," Beamer said. Of course.

So Beamer and I (there's a phrase I never thought I'd say) trudged up the beach. And I tried to shake off the sinking feeling I got as we walked away from Sebastian and Anna, lying side by side. I tried even harder to dismiss the visual of Sebastian leaning over Anna and kissing her, and the knot that visual was weaving in my stomach. Because Anna seemed happy. And I had told her it was okay. Which meant it had to be.

That didn't mean I had to be okay with getting stuck with Beamer, did it?

As soon as we were out of earshot of the others, he turned to me, a serious look on his face. "Listen, about the other night—"

"Forget about it," I said, cutting him off.

"Nah, Maisie, I wanted to explain—"

"There's nothing to explain."

"There is," he said. "I wanted to explain that spending time with you—it wasn't some trick or plan to allow Seb to get some action."

"Ha. Like that's not what's happening right now?"

"No, that's *not* what's happening right now," he said, frustration seeping into his voice.

"It's fine—I told Anna she should be with Sebastian," I said.

He raised his eyebrows in surprise. "But I thought—"

"If they like each other, I'm not going to get in their way. I'm over him, anyway."

Beamer snorted as he passed in front of me. We had reached the outdoor shower and tap at the end of the path.

"Looks like you and I are gonna be stuck with each other, hey," I said with resignation.

I couldn't see Beamer's face, and he didn't say anything as he stood under the shower, rinsing the salt and sand off his body. I looked away, waiting for my turn at the tap. I just needed to rinse off my feet.

Cold water splashed my side. I squealed and turned back to see Beamer grinning wickedly. He laughed when he saw the murderous expression on my face.

"It's like you said, Maisie Martin: you're stuck with me."

I let out an irritated cry and walked away as quickly as I could. He jogged to catch up, still dripping wet. His towel was flung around his shoulders, and he ran one end through his hair as he smiled at me. He opened his mouth, and I expected an apology— however insincere it might be—but all he said was, "So, *The Scorpion King*, *San Andreas*, or *Central Intelligence*?"

"What?"

"Which do you want to watch first?" He sniffed and wiped at his face with the towel.

I remembered our argument from the other night. "Beamer, you're not going to convince me that The Rock is the greatest action star of all time, so you may as well just drop it now. You're wrong, and you have terrible opinions."

"Prove it," he said with a grin.

We made a deal. I'm going to show him three Arnold Schwarzenegger movies, and he'll show me three of The Rock's. We'll each rate them according to five important criteria: quotable lines, overall entertainment value, explosions, timelessness, and action hero-ness (which is kinda like *je ne sais quoi* in that it's a distinctive quality that's hard to describe). We have to be fair. And at the end of the experiment, the person whose champion has the least amount of points loses and has to take a punishment of the winner's choosing.

It's really, really important that I win, 'cos I can only imagine what sick monstrosities Beamer's mind would conjure up.

We grabbed lunch and went back to the cabin, starting off with *Terminator 2: Judgment Day*, which Beamer had never seen (just shows you how unqualified his opinion truly is). We agreed to keep our scores private until we've made it through all the movies, to ensure it's a fair competition.

I gotta admit, it was pretty fun. I mean, you can't really go wrong with *T2*, and it helps that you have to stay pretty silent while watching a movie, so my Beamer Tolerance Threshold remained in the safe zone. Even when he injected his own commentary over key scenes, I didn't mind, because I could tell he was enjoying it (I swear, as Arnie gave that last thumbs-up at the end, I glanced over at Beamer and he had tears in his eyes). I'm totally gonna win this thing.

We only got through the one movie before Sebastian and Anna walked in, all sunshiney and giggly, and Anna announced she was *not* sitting through any action movies when it was still so beautiful outside. The four of us went for a walk, Sebastian and Anna leading the way. Sebastian started up a game of "Would You Rather" that included highly intellectual questions like "Would you rather never find love, or get married to your soul mate but have to wear a vest made of their pubes every day?" (it'd have to be the pube vest, obviously), and "Would you rather pee every time you laugh, or have your eyeball pop out every time you sneeze?" (I chose pee laughter.)

At dinner, Sebastian made a big show of getting Anna a drink and passing her food and generally being oh-so-attentive. It made all the adults exchange looks, but that didn't seem to bother Sebastian. He only stirred when Kane, cackling with glee, said, "Sebby, is Anna your *girlfriend* now?" and Lincoln started making smooching noises. Their laughter soon turned to screams when Sebastian got them both in a headlock. He didn't let go until his dad said something to him in Hokkien that made all three brothers settle down real quick.

When Sebastian returned to his seat, he and Anna shared a look that felt so intimate, I was almost embarrassed for them.

Still. It was nice to see Anna so happy. Really, it was.

Thursday, 21 December

1 thing I discovered today:

1. I think my parents might be headed for a divorce.

Evidence: This article I found when I googled "how to know if your parents are going to get a divorce."

* * *

Look, I didn't really think my parents were in that much trouble. I mean, sure, the amount they've been fighting and/or not talking lately has been kinda freaking me out. I kept telling myself it'd blow over. But Dad hasn't been answering my calls the past couple of days. When I mentioned it to Mum, her lips went all tight and she muttered he was busy working, but I could tell she was holding something back.

I finally got through to Dad today, and...he was really cheery. For a moment I considered I'd just been overthinking everything. But then Dad asked to be put on to Mum, and she said she couldn't talk right then—because she was painting her nails. The disappointment in Dad's voice when I relayed the message was like a punch to the gut.

When I hung up the phone, I turned to Dr. Google, expecting the results to tell me, "Don't be silly, Maisie! Your parents love each other! Everyone goes through rough patches, they'll be fine!" But what actually came up was this article, "8 Interesting Signs Your Parents Might Get Divorced" (although I don't know what's so INTERESTING about it). And it was things like, oh, you know, avoiding talking to each other, spending long hours at work, going on separate vacations, taking extra interest in their appearances...

...

...

...

DJ, ARE MY PARENTS GETTING A DIVORCE?

I know what you're going to say. Why am I asking you? What would you know? Nothing, except what I tell you, of course.

I guess I could ask Laura. Mum tells her everything.

Or, you know, I could just ask my parents.

But I don't think I will, DJ.

Because I don't think I want to know the answer. Not really.

Instead, I'll do what any healthy, well-adjusted sixteen-year-old would do. I'll bury my worries deep, deep down, and use copious amounts of alcohol to forget they exist.

Kidding! I'll just drown them out with terrible movies and other assorted fun. Today, for instance, I watched *Fast Five* with Beamer (I've seen it before and I'd never admit it to him, but it's pretty great), and I dragged my butt to the beach with the others not once but *twice*. I didn't go in the water, of course. But I was there. Tonight, we all played Monopoly. (Anna won. She's viciously competitive when it comes to games. So is Sebastian; he sulked for a good few minutes like the sore loser he is—but then Anna's kisses cheered him up considerably.)

As for me, not a worry was to be found. No siree, none from me. *Hakuna Matata*. No worries. None about my parents. None about Sebastian and Anna. Especially none about my sister, who—did I mention?—is arriving tomorrow. None at all.

Friday, 22 December

3 things I discovered today:

1. FORGET WHAT I SAID ABOUT NO WORRIES. I AM ALL WORRIES. IN FACT, I'M IN WHAT YOU MIGHT CALL A PICKLE, IF YOU WERE A NINETY-FIVE-YEAR-OLD NAMED BERYL.

Evidence: A surprising phone call I received today.

2. My sister is the biggest hypocrite in the world.

Evidence: Her actions do not match her words. Not even close.

3. People have really strong opinions about ketchup.

Evidence: It's the kind of debate that divides friends. Nations.

* * *

Oh god. Oh god. Oh god.

I feel like Anakin Skywalker in *Revenge of the Sith.*
"What have I done? What have I dooonnnne?"

Let me go back to the start. Another morning at
the beach (if you're wondering: yes, I'm sick of it, but
apparently I'm the only one).

Everyone was in the water, and I was lying on the
sand—stewing in my own juices as per usual—listening to my mega movie scores playlist (it relaxes
me, okay?). All of a sudden, Leila's grinning face was
above me.

"Hey, babe, I thought that was you," she said as I
pulled my earphones out and sat up. She pointed
to her group of friends about sixty feet away and
insisted I join them.

"Oh, I don't want to intrude," I said.

"Don't be silly! Everyone wants to meet you." She
was already walking away, so I scrambled up to follow
her. I glanced out to where Anna's head was bobbing
in the water, waved to try to get her attention and
then pointed toward Leila to indicate I was moving.
She waved back, so I assumed she got the message.

Leila's friends were spread out on towels in an
informal semicircle, a packet of chips open between

them, alongside an iPhone hooked up to portable speakers playing Flume.

"Maisie, meet the crew." Leila gestured to a girl with dark hair piled on top of her head and glasses framing her dark eyes. "This is Jo, she's the smartest person I know. She's gonna change the world one day."

Jo rolled her eyes, but smiled and waved at me.

Leila pointed to a white guy with brown tousled hair and big lips, who was lying on his side propped up on his elbow next to a pretty girl with the longest hair I've ever seen. "That's Will and Hannah; they're sickeningly cute, but not terrible people if you can ever get them apart," Leila said.

Will stuck his finger up at her and Hannah threw a chip in her direction. They both said "hey" to me.

Leila gestured to the last person in the group, a skinny guy wearing a wide-brimmed hat. "And this is Kieron, the bane of my existence."

He blew Leila a kiss and smiled at me. "Help yourself," he said, gesturing to the chips as Leila sat down and I kneeled beside her.

"You're just in time to help us settle a debate," Will said, speaking with his mouth full. "Does ketchup belong in the fridge or the cupboard?"

"Um...the fridge?" I said.

Will groaned, but Jo let out a "yussss" of victory and said, "See! I told you! It says right there on the bottle: *Refrigerate after opening!*"

"Well my mum has been putting it in the cupboard my whole life, and it's never done me any damage," Will said.

"That we know of," Jo shot back.

"Guys. Come on. There's only one place it belongs," Leila said.

The others looked at her expectantly.

"In the trash."

"Mate, that's sacrilegious," said Will.

"*Mate*," Leila said, lacing it with meaning—that meaning being, *Shut up, you'll never win this.*

They traded insults back and forth for a while until Hannah said, "Alright, change of subject, please," which got them onto the topic of the "epic" party happening at Will's place on Christmas Eve.

"You should come, Maisie," Leila said. "It'll be fun. Bring the others too."

"Oh, no—I mean, I wouldn't want to intrude."

"There you go again. You wouldn't be. Right, Will?"

Will was quiet for a moment.

"It's okay, really, don't worry about it," I said.

"Look, I'm not gonna lie to you, Maisie—I don't like it," said Will, scratching his chin.

Hannah elbowed him in the stomach.

"Ow! What? It's not my fault the woman has terrible opinions about ketchup. I mean, I might invite her into my house and my sauce would somehow mysteriously end up in the fridge, and then who would I have to blame but myself for letting an enemy into my territory?"

"Ignore him, Maisie. He's just being a dick. You're definitely coming," said Jo.

"Hey, nah, you can't say that, you're one of them! You're not invited either," Will protested, trying to keep a straight face and failing.

"But you're coming, right, Maisie?" The question came from Hannah.

"Of course she is," Will said, tossing a chip into his mouth. "I was kidding, in case that wasn't obvious."

All eyes were on me.

"Um...I'll have to check with my friends, if that's cool," I said. *And my mum*, I thought.

"Sure, no worries," Will said cheerily.

They started talking about plans for the night, and I was sitting there listening, trying to be as still and quiet as possible so they wouldn't regret asking me to join them, let alone inviting me to their party, when my phone rang. I didn't recognize the number and was planning to ignore it, but Leila turned to me and said, "Are you going to answer that?" I smiled and pressed the green button.

"Hello?"

"Hello, this is Janice from the Cobbers Bay Miss Teen Queen pageant. I'm calling for a Maisie Martin?"

Shit.

"Um, this is her, I mean she, I mean me," I choked out. *Shiiiiiiiiiit.*

"Wonderful! Maisie, we've received your application and we'd like to congratulate you on being accepted to compete in this year's pageant, to take place at the Paradise Hotel on Saturday, the sixth of January. The entry fee of one hundred and ninety-nine dollars is due by December thirty-first. A free participator's trophy is included in the cost!"

"Um..."

"If you have any questions or concerns, please let me know. You have my number now. We look forward to seeing you on the day!"

"Okay..." I said. My head was spinning.

"Bye now. Have a great day," Janice said in her chirpy voice, and hung up.

I stared at the phone, frozen in horror.

"Babe, are you okay?" Leila asked.

I slowly raised my head to look at her, my eyes wide.

"Who was that? Is everything alright?"

What have I done? What have I dooooooone?

"That...that was the pageant. They were calling to congratulate me on the acceptance of my entry."

Leila screamed and jumped up, grabbing my hands and pulling me up with her. I dimly registered some of the others cheering.

"Oh my god, this is amazing," Leila was saying, bouncing up and down, still holding on to my hands. When I didn't match her enthusiasm, she stopped and peered into my eyes. "This is amazing, right?"

I just stared at her, unable to speak. I was feeling so many things at once that I felt nothing at all. My body, my brain, everything was blank.

"Hey, let's take a walk," Leila said after a minute of me standing there like I was playing a one-woman game of stuck-in-the-mud. She tucked her arm through mine and pulled me along. As we walked, my thoughts slowly spilled out of me. I told her how I couldn't believe I'd actually been selected. That it must be some kind of joke. What were they playing at? I couldn't do it. I couldn't stand up on stage. In an evening dress. *In a bikini.* I didn't have any talent. It would be humiliating.

Leila listened to it all, and then she said, very gently, "But, babe, I thought there was a part of you that really wants this?"

I swallowed, but didn't say anything.

She smiled as she turned us both around and we headed back toward the others. "I reckon you'll be brilliant. But it's up to you. Just think about it, alright?"

I shook my head. "There's no way I can take part in that pageant."

* * *

Oh god. I'm taking part in the pageant.

You're probably wondering what made me do this one-eighty. To be honest, I still feel really sick about it all. But this afternoon, something happened to change my mind. Guess who was here when we got back from the beach?

Well, you don't have to guess, since I already told you she was arriving today. Yep. It was none other than my darling big sister, Eva.

She had her new girlfriend in tow. Her name is Bess. She seems really nice. Has a great laugh. This amazing pinup girl style. Lots of tattoos.

Oh, and she's really fat.

I'm not saying that to be mean or bitchy. It's just a fact.

She's fat. Like I'm fat. We're fat!

You know who's not fat?

You know who *hates* fat people?

EVA. My beautiful, *darling* sister. The one who—who—

Who is the biggest effing hypocrite I have ever met in my life.

There she was, acting as sweet as a cinnamon cronut—*Oh, Maisie, it's so good to see you, why didn't you write back to my emails? I'm so happy you're finally meeting Bess, I've been telling her all about you. Won't this be an awesome vacation? It's a shame Dad's not here, but it'll be nice to have some girl time, hey?*

And there was Mum, all teary-eyed, hugging and squeezing Eva like she hasn't seen her in years (I mean, it's only been six months), and hugging and squeezing Bess like she was a long-lost daughter too, and saying, *Yes, yes now that the whole family is here, we can truly have a wonderful vacation.*

And something inside of me just snapped (spoiler: pretty sure it was my brain).

I stood there, staring at them, and before I could even register what I was saying, my mouth was blurting out, "Yes! We *are* going to have a wonderful vacation. I'm going to be in the Miss Teen Queen pageant—and who knows? I might even win!"

Mum and Eva stared at me with a look on their

faces for which the technical term is, I believe, thunderstruck. Anna looked confused. Bess looked clueless. Oh, she had nooo idea.

"Maisie, what are you talking about?" Eva said.

"I didn't know you'd entered," Mum said.

"Oh yeah. The other day."

"Well, that's wonderful, Missy-May. I'm proud of you for having the courage."

I could tell Mum was choosing her words very carefully. Not carefully enough, though.

"What's that supposed to mean?" I said.

Eva and Mum exchanged a look. Anna was watching us all with wary eyes. Now Bess was the one looking confused.

Eva stepped toward me and put a hand on my arm. So sweet. So sympathetic. So fake. She said, "You know, it's a really tough competition. Don't worry if you don't get a call back. It's great that you entered."

God, I can feel the rage bubbling up inside me all over again just writing this. It's still nothing on what I felt in that moment, though. I wanted to slap her. I didn't. Instead I said: "It just so happens I got a phone call today. I'm going to be in the Miss Teen Queen pageant in two weeks. You're not the only one in this family who can achieve anything, you know."

And I spun around and rushed out the door.

When I reached the sand dunes, I crumpled on the ground and pulled out my phone, sending one text message.

Me: *I'm in. Do you still want to dress me?*

Leila: *YAAAAAAAAASSS QUEEEEEEN.*

Saturday, 23 December

1 thing I discovered today:

1. It turns out people have strong feelings about me entering this pageant.

Evidence: The conversations I had about it with literally everyone today. See status report.

* * *

Status report:

Dad: Weirded out, cautiously supportive, totally absent. ("I thought you hated that thing? Oh, okay, if it's what you want, that's great, Eminem...No, I don't think I'll make it there for the pageant. Sorry, honey. Work is still hectic and, you know, it's such a long way for a short period of time. We've talked about all this already. That's why I won't be there for Christmas. How's your mother?")

Mum: Concerned, embarrassed. ("Are you sure this is what you want, Missy-May? I'm just...worried, that's all. I mean, you don't even wear your swimsuit on the beach. How are you going to wear it on stage? No, no, that's not what I meant. No, Maisie, I'm not embarrassed. I want you to be happy. I'm worried this will make you—of course, if it's what you want. Is it really what you want?")

Laura: Supportive. ("Good on you, Maisie, you'll be fabulous! We'll make a day of it like we did when Eva was in it.")

Jimmy: Supportive-by-default. ("Reckon your old man will make the trip after all? Oh well, we'll be there!")

The twins: Bored.

("Do we have to go?")

("No way! It'll be boooorrring.")

Anna: Concerned. ("Maisie, are you sure about this? I mean, you don't even wear your swimsuit on the beach. How are you going to wear them on stage? No, I don't think you're making a mistake. I'm just surprised. But it'll be fun. If it's what you want.")

Sebastian: Supportive(?). ("Nice one, Maise. You gonna do your Wookiee impression?")

Beamer: Lecherous. ("Well, well, well, aren't you full of surprises! Gonna need any help backstage? I volunteer as tribute. Ow, stop whacking me!")

Leila: Enthusiastic. ("Babe, I've got so many ideas! Let me do your measurements. Don't be embarrassed! C'mon. This is going to be fun. Don't worry about a thing. You're going to be really beautiful. Okay, look...you've still got time to back out, right? When do you have to pay the registration fee by? The thirty-first? Why don't you start prepping, and if you still feel sick about it all by then, you don't have to do it. Just call them up and say you won't be entering after all. But hey, you might be really excited by then. Honestly, I think it'll be great. Just you wait!")

Eva: I don't know, and I don't care. She and Bess headed to their Airbnb last night (she's too good for the RV park now), and I avoided her today. I think she and Bess had a fight, because things seemed really tense when I did see them, but to find out what happened would imply that I care. Which I don't.

Me: Shitting bricks. I mean, I don't even wear my swimsuit on the beach. How am I going to wear it on stage?!?!

Sunday, 24 December

2 things I discovered today:

1. Shopping on Christmas Eve is the fourth layer of hell.

Evidence: I went with Anna to buy some "last min-ute" presents (translation: she wanted something for Sebastian. Does that mean they're getting seri-ous already?! She bought him a t-shirt, in case you're wondering).

2. Mum has either been possessed by an alien or turned into a Stepford robot.

Evidence: She's being really nice. She's totally fine with us going to this party tonight and even bought us a four-pack of wine coolers to split "as long as that's all you drink. *And* you have to be home by mid-night." (Lol, okay, Mum.)

That's all I've got today, DJ. It's pretty early, so who knows, maybe I'll "discover" something at this party tonight, but I figured I better get something down here beforehand, because I don't plan on being in a fit state to do so later. It's alright—Mum will be so pissed herself she won't even notice. Eva and Bess are keeping an eye on the twins, which means the old people are free to go out and "get hammered." Forget about a minimum drinking age, there needs to be a maximum drinking age. People over the age of thirty-five should have more dignity. It's embarrassing to us all.

Monday, 25 December

2 things I discovered today:

1. Prawns are not worth eating unless you can get some-one else to peel them for you.

Evidence: The mess on my fingers and the ten thousand years it took to get one prawn ready to eat. (Dad usually peels them for me.)

2. Sometimes, viewing something from someone else's perspective can have very unintended consequences.

Evidence: Oh boy. I need a lot more space for this. See below.

Merry Christmas, DJ! If you celebrate Christmas, that is. Sorry, I shouldn't make assumptions about your life.

I've come into my room to have a nap—well, that's what I told the others, anyway. Everyone's in a post-lunch food coma frame of mind, but mine is buzzing and I've just got to empty it out or it might explode.

Now I'm here, though, I don't know where to begin.

I guess a good place would be the party. That's where shit went down.

Honestly, it was like no party I've ever been to. For starters, Will's house is MASSIVE, with this huge deck and an infinity pool that overlooks the beach. His parents must be loaded. They were there, but I didn't meet them, because they stayed upstairs the whole time like actual good, non-painful parents. Guess who else was there? Like, the whole population of Cobbers Bay between the ages of sixteen and eighteen.

It was like those parties you see in teen movies, where there are people everywhere, sipping from red cups, dancing, making out, playing party games— you know, the kind that make you say, "No party is actually like that."

Except this one was. Minus the red cups (we had white ones instead).

When we got there, Leila screamed and ran over to give me a hug before turning to greet the others. She gave us a whirlwind tour ("Drinks over there and there and there—food over there and here—isn't this place so extra?—bathroom's down there—guest bedrooms down here if you want to get changed and go for a swim or, you know, whatever.").

"I didn't realize this was a pool party," I said.

"It's not! I mean, it's a party, there's a pool...don't worry, I'm not going in. Well, not yet at least. It took me way too long to look this good to undo it all already."

We deposited our drinks in one of the many ice chests. Leila introduced us to a bunch of people from her school whose names I didn't quite catch. I was relieved when we spotted Kieron and Jo sitting with a few others, chatting on a large U-shaped outdoor sofa near the pool.

"Where's Will and Hannah?" I asked.

"Oh, they're, uh, getting changed," Leila said breezily. She grabbed my arm and leaned in to whisper, "That's Alex. The guy I told you about? No, don't look! Okay, slowly. He's sitting next to Kieron."

I glanced at the guy she'd pointed out (subtly,

subtly). "He's cute," I said, because he was. He was kinda pointy-looking—his nose, his chin—but it somehow added to his appeal. When Leila introduced us, he actually stood up and shook our hands. Leila laughed and started teasing him, while I sat down on the other side of Kieron. Beamer plonked down next to me. It was only then I realized that Sebastian and Anna weren't with us anymore.

"Where'd they...?"

"I think they went to *get changed*," Beamer said.

"But none of us brought swimsuits," I said, and he looked at me as if to say, *C'mon, really?*

I took a big gulp of my drink and turned to chat to Kieron, trying to clear the unwelcome image that had crashed through my mind. It was going well until Beamer brought up the subject of our movie challenge, and Kieron said, "Why bother? The Rock is obviously gonna win."

Beamer hooted triumphantly. I couldn't believe it.

"Arnold Schwarzenegger is a legend," I said, unable to stop my voice from rising just a little.

"When was the last time he even made a good movie?" Kieron said.

"It doesn't matter when they were made. People are still watching them today."

"Huh. You know, I can't say I've really seen any

except that 'It's not a tumor' one." Kieron put on a terrible Schwarzenegger voice to quote *Kindergarten Cop*.

"WHAT?"

"Oooh, you've done it now," Beamer said. "Look at that. I swear that vein in her forehead is going to burst."

I clapped my hand to my head, and they both laughed. I glared at Beamer before turning back to Kieron. "I'm going to write you a list to watch. Hand me your phone."

Kieron looked at me like I was a total weirdo, but obeyed. Beamer chuckled and got up to refill our drinks.

Kieron had his head in close to mine, leaning over to see what I was writing in the notes app on his phone. He looked up as Beamer walked away and said quietly to me, "So what's the deal with you two?"

"What do you mean?" I said, not looking up.

"Like, are you together?"

That made me look up. "What?! No! Ew."

Kieron furrowed his brows. "Don't look so horrified. He's hot!"

"Beamer?!"

"Yeeeeeah. Oh, shhh, here he comes." Louder, he said, "God, how long is this list?"

"Mate, she'll be here all night," Beamer said, setting our drinks down on the glass coffee table in front of us. As he told Kieron what I'd made him watch so far (we'd done *True Lies* the day before) and they discussed which Rock movie he should make me watch next, I acted like I was still typing on Kieron's phone, but really I was trying to look at Beamer without him noticing. Trying to see him as Kieron might—as a stranger might. With fresh eyes.

And what did I see? Oh, you know...a guy with broad shoulders and biceps that popped as he twisted open a drink. A butt that filled his jeans nicely as he bent over in front of me to pass a drink to Leila. Light brown hair that was messy, but the kind of boy-messy that looks good. A well-shaped nose, and pink lips he unconsciously bit down on as he listened to Kieron talk. Dark brown eyes that looked almost black in the fading light as he—as he looked over at me.

Shit. I ducked my head down quickly. I'd forgotten to be subtle and had been flat-out staring.

He'd seen me.

But worst of all, I'd seen him.

Kieron was right. Beamer *is* hot.

I'd like to state on the record that everything that happened later is all Kieron's fault.

Wait. Someone's coming.

* * *

Oh my god. Things keep getting weirder and weirder.

It's nighttime now. Everyone is in bed. This afternoon—wait. I need to explain about last night first. Let's not get ahead of ourselves.

So, last night.

We were playing Truth or Dare, because we were in full cliché mode and enjoying every second of it. Anna and Sebastian had resurfaced by this stage, and Will and Hannah had appeared ("Do I need to check on my ketchup?" was the first thing Will said to me).

Anna had been dared by some random guy named Tom to go in the water in her bra and undies.

"You're disgusting," Jo said to him with a sneer.

"It's alright," Anna said. "Doesn't show any more than my swimsuit."

She stood up and stripped off, right there in front of everyone. She was wearing a purple satin bra and matching undies. She was right. It didn't show any more than her swimsuit. I still couldn't help feeling a little shocked. Beside her, Sebastian seemed pretty shocked himself. He looked over at Beamer, eyes wide and eyebrows raised, as if to say, *Is this for real?* Beamer had a similar look on his face.

She marched over to the pool steps and walked in, submerging herself to shoulder height and then spinning around, a self-satisfied smile on her face. Everyone clapped and cheered. She climbed the steps to get out, saying, "Quite refreshing, actually."

"Heads up," Will called, chucking Anna a towel.

She wrapped it around herself and sat back down next to Sebastian, opposite me on the U-shaped lounge.

"Alright, my turn. Sebastian," she said, turning to him with a smile, "truth or dare?"

He smiled back at her. "Truth."

"Hmmm...who was your first kiss?"

Sebastian licked his lips and stared off into the distance for a moment. A jolt ran through me when he turned and his eyes locked on mine. He pointed at me with a grin and said, "Maisie Martin."

"What?!" Anna and I both said at the same time. She looked from him to me with confusion.

"Aw, don't tell me you don't remember, Maise. You'll break my heart," he said.

A vision of us getting "married" at five years old flashed in my head. Eva, the "celebrant," had said, "Now you guys have to kiss." We'd both leaned in and joined our lips in the quickest peck of all time, before promptly wiping them with the backs of our hands and giggling.

I rolled my eyes and shook my head at Sebastian, who told the story to the others. "So I guess Maisie and I are married," he finished.

"Oh my god, now that I think about it, I'm pretty sure I married my second cousin when I was four," Leila said.

"I married the girl next door," Kieron said with a laugh.

"Are we still playing or what?" Anna broke in. "Sebastian, it's your turn. Who are you going to pick?"

"Hmmm." He glanced my way and my heart sped up, but then his eyes settled next to me. "Beamer."

"Here we go." Beamer chose dare, and Sebastian gazed around as if searching for an idea. He looked from Anna to the pool and then back at Beamer, a smirk appearing on his face.

"Mate, if you wanna see me in my underwear, you just have to ask," Beamer said.

"Naaah, that'd be too easy. I wanna see you naked."

I nearly spat out my drink. Beamer chuckled and stood up, walking over to the edge of the pool. He faced us as he reached up and pulled his shirt off from behind his neck in that way all guys seem genetically programmed to do. A few girls catcalled and Kieron whistled. I tried not to notice that V of muscle leading into Beamer's jeans.

Shucking his shoes off and starting to unzip his fly, he turned around so he was facing the pool, his back to the crowd. In one swift movement, his jeans and undies were off, his bare, very white butt on display for a split second before he dive-bombed into the pool. Cheers erupted around me and then Will was standing up, pulling his own shirt off.

"What are you doing?" Hannah cried.

"Can't let the poor sucker go it alone," Will said, and pretty quickly his butt was on display before he too jumped in. Alex followed, along with a couple of other guys, and soon the pool was a veritable sausage soup.

Jo and Leila scooched up next to me and Kieron, laughing and shaking their heads.

"What is it with guys and getting their dicks out?" Jo said.

"Come on, Sebby, you started this," Beamer called out.

Sebastian ran his hands over his face and groaned, but he was smiling, and then he was standing up and tugging his shirt off and—oh god. I couldn't look.

But I couldn't *not* look.

"You going in?" I said to Kieron. I tried to keep my voice smooth, but there was definite squeakage involved.

"Nah, I'm good right here."

I heard a squeal and turned to see Anna, along with a few other girls who had stripped to their underwear, hitting the water with a splash.

"I am way too sober for this," Jo said, standing up. "You guys want a drink?"

I shook my head. I was feeling lightly buzzed but didn't particularly want to get out of control. Kieron got up and followed her inside, and Leila slid closer to me.

"I swear, Will's parties aren't always like this," she said, as Will climbed out of the pool and ran over to Hannah, picking her up and jumping back in the water with her. She screamed on the way in and gasped when she resurfaced, splashing him angrily before breaking into giggles.

"They're usually not so naked, at least," Leila added.

"I've seen more penises tonight than I have in my entire life," I whispered.

"Oh my god, I saw Alex's. I don't know if I can sustain my crush now... What?! Don't look at me like that. You know what I mean! Some things are best left to the imagination. Not that I was imagining it." She covered her face with her hands.

When our giggles had subsided, I looked around. I noticed there was light around the edges of one of the upstairs windows, but the blinds were down. Still, if Will's parents chose this moment to look out... "Don't Will's parents care?"

Leila shrugged. "They're not regular parents, they're cool parents," she said, with an exaggerated wink. "Like Amy Poehler in *Mean Girls*."

"Ah, I love that movie!"

We talked about the many wonders of *Mean Girls* for a little while. People started getting out of the pool, and once again there was far too much flesh in my line of sight. I half laughed, half groaned. Leila cupped her hand to her eyes, blocking her peripheral vision, and I did the same.

Nudging me, she said, "Hey, have you been thinking about the pageant?"

I slid down and rested my head against the back of the lounge, sighing. Maybe it was because I was tipsy. Maybe it was just the weirdness of the night. Maybe it was because I knew I could trust Leila. But I finally admitted the truth.

"You know what? I really, really want to do it." I scrunched up my face, embarrassed to have said the words out loud.

"Yessss! That's what I like to hear. You're not going to regret it."

"I wouldn't be so sure. I mean, I want to do it—but I still don't see how I can."

"We'll work on that. Trust me. I'll have you feeling like a million bucks."

I snorted. Then, quietly, I said, "I'm scared, Leila."

She put a comforting hand on my arm. "That's how you know something is worth doing."

Beamer chose that moment to reappear and plant himself next to me. He had a towel wrapped around his hips, but his chest was bare and still covered in droplets ofwater. He ran his hands back and forth through his hair, causing it to stick up in all directions. He lay back on the chair, his head a few centimeters from mine.

I sat up and moved forward, perching on the edge of the seat. "God, Beamer, put some clothes on."

"Hey, I'm going to find out where the others disappeared to," Leila said, walking away before I'd even registered what she was saying. I looked around and realized nearly everyone had gone inside. There were some randoms talking quietly together at the other end of the pool, and a couple in the corner making out. I couldn't see Sebastian and Anna anywhere. I was about to get up and follow Leila inside when Beamer reached out and tapped my shoulder.

"Hey, Maisie Martin," he said. He kept poking me until I turned to look at him. He had a lazy smile on his face.

"Yes, pest?" I replied, trying to ignore the weird way my heart was beating and the dry feeling in my throat as I looked into his dark eyes.

"Truth or dare?" he said.

I rolled my eyes. "The game's over, Beamer."

"Come on, I didn't get my go. I wanted to ask you something."

"Don't you know enough of my truths already?"

"No way. But you could always choose dare."

I raised an eyebrow. "Fine. Dare."

"I dare you," he said, grinning and punctuating every word with a gentle prod of my shoulder, "to kiss me."

I made a scoffing noise and shook my head, turning away from him.

"Knew you wouldn't do it."

I just want to reiterate that I blame Kieron entirely for what happened next. If he hadn't planted the idea in my head that Beamer was anything other than a pain in my arse, I never would have done it.

Well, I'm pretty sure I wouldn't have.

But I did.

I spun around and launched myself at Beamer's mouth. He froze for a moment, but then his lips were moving against mine. His hands were roaming up and down my back, over my shoulders, my neck, into my hair. I reached up and cupped his face with my hands, not breaking the kiss. Not thinking about anything except briefly registering that he was much better than I expected him to be. Not that I expected him to be anything, because that would imply I'd thought about it. Which I hadn't. I swear. But if I had, I would've thought he'd have some terrible washing machine-style tongue action like Ryan Rodriguez did when I kissed him under the bleachers after school in Year 9.

Beamer's tongue action...well, look, I'm not going to go into details because it will probably sound way less hot than it was, but let's just say it was not like a washing machine.

Wait, did I just say it was hot?

Yes. Yes I did.

Because it was.

Oh god, it was.

What's wrong with me?

I don't know how long we'd been kissing when all of a sudden Beamer broke off, pushing me away and leaning forward, resting his elbows on his knees and his face in his hands. He let out an irritated groan.

I sat there for a second in shock, staring at his back. He didn't move. "You know, if you didn't want to kiss me, you shouldn't have dared me," I spat out, then I got up and rushed inside.

I heard him calling after me, but he didn't follow and I didn't look back.

Tuesday, 26 December

2 things I discovered today:

1. Do not get in the way of Leila at a fabric sale.

Evidence: Leila and I went to this giant fabric warehouse to pick out material for the pageant. She was a woman on a mission in there.

2. I finally get why people make out during movies.

Evidence: ;););)

* * *

Ah, Boxing Day. When you have two choices of activity: watching the cricket or shopping the sales (aka the third layer of hell).

"Let's go with your mum and the others," Anna said this morning. They were heading to the mall. But I'd already made plans with Leila.

"Sorry, I thought you'd be hanging out with Sebastian," I said.

She pulled a face. "He's watching the cricket."

"Do you want to come with us?"

Anna considered it for a moment. "Nah, I wouldn't want to get in the way."

I told her she wouldn't be, but she said, "It's alright. I'll convince Seb there are more interesting things to do than watch cricket. It shouldn't be too hard."

Mum's words from yesterday drifted into my head. As I'd helped her prepare the salad for lunch, she'd whispered to me, "What's going on with you and Anna?"

"What? Nothing."

"Something seems...off between you two. She seems to spend more time with Seb than she does with you. I thought—"

"Everything's fine, Mum," I'd said.

But was it?

I shoved the thought away. Of course it was.

* * *

Leila had assured me shopping a fabric sale on Boxing Day was not, in fact, the third layer of hell, but actual heaven. And while I wouldn't quite go that far, I have to admit it wasn't any layer of hell. It wasn't even purgatory. It was just...fun.

There were people everywhere, sure, and the place was kind of a mess, but seeing it through Leila's eyes, it was like a treasure hunt, and she knew exactly where to start digging.

"This. This is *perfect*," Leila said as she held up a roll of soft material with a bright floral print. I reached out to touch the fabric. Now *that* was heavenly.

"It's lovely," I said, and she let out a small squeal. "But—"

"No! No buts! I won't hear any buts. It's perfect, I'm telling you."

"But—"

"What did I say?"

"Okay, bu—I mean...look, what about this one? That will suit my skin tone better, don't you think?" I pointed to a roll of black fabric.

"No, I don't think. *This* one will look beautiful on you. You can't hide behind black forever, you know. And don't even think about looking at the navy." She

136

picked up the roll of fabric to take it to the counter, then paused. Looking over her shoulder at me she said, "Wait, babe. I'm sorry. If this is going to make you uncomfortable, I'll find something else. Just tell me to shut up when I get too bossy."

I walked over to examine the fabric once again. I touched it and smiled. "You know what? You're the expert. Let's do it."

She grinned. "You won't regret it!"

"You keep saying that. But I do so many things I end up regretting."

"Like what?" She wasn't really paying attention to me as she told the shop assistant how much material we needed.

"Like kissing Beamer."

That got her attention.

"What?! At the party?! I knew it. I *knew* there was something going on between you two. I was getting a vibe. Why do you think I made myself scarce? You're welcome, by the way. But wait—why do you regret it? What happened?"

"Well, for starters, it's *Beamer*. You're wrong about something going on between us. We kind of hate each other."

She gave me a look.

"It's true! Honestly, I think the only pleasure he gets from my company is annoying me."

"And kissing you," she said with a smirk. "Seriously babe, that's how all the best romances start out. Look at Gilbert Blythe and Anne Shirley. Or...Han Solo and Princess Leia! It's all about the flirty banter."

I didn't respond immediately because I had to pay for the fabric (it was coming out of the Christmas money I'd received—Mum had said, "I thought you could get something for the pageant—maybe we can go shopping tomorrow?" Like I'd voluntarily submit to that torture). It gave me a moment to consider Leila's words. *Was* Beamer flirting with me? Worse—was I flirting with him?

A quick succession of images flashed through my head: Beamer snapping my swimsuit straps, water-bombing me, poking me, teasing me; me telling him to shut up, whacking him, asking him to leave me alone; Sebastian and I getting "married," playing together, me reading his poetry, me getting heart palpitations just being near him, his smile... yeah, nah, it was definitely not a *thing* with Beamer. Sebastian was my Han Solo. The Beamer incident—it was purely because of what Kieron had said. It had made me curious. That was all. I told Leila as much.

Except...except...

"Except it happened again yesterday."

"WHAT?! What do you mean?! Tell me everything."

So I told her. I guess I should tell you too, DJ.

Remember when I said someone was coming? Yeah, that was Beamer.

I'd been avoiding him all day. Like, more than usual. After storming away from him the night before, I'd grabbed Anna as soon as I saw her and told her I wanted to get home before Mum cracked the shits. Despite her protests, I'd dragged her out of there without waiting for the guys. I was *not* ready to face whatever the hell had happened with Beamer.

Christmas morning was just our family—except Dad, of course. I Skyped with him and he said how much he was missing us, and that Grandma was really excited to "finally be able to celebrate with some family, at least," which is her passive-aggressive way of complaining once again that we go away every Christmas (it's always bugged her). I handed Dad over to Eva, but she hung up after she was done without even trying to pass him on to Mum. I don't think the two of them have spoken at all since we got here. But when Mum gave me my Christmas card (containing my Christmas cash), it said "Love, Mum and Dad," so I took that as a sign they're still together and absolutely not getting divorced—on paper, at least. Until they tell me otherwise. That's what I'm focusing on.

For lunch we gathered in the picnic area near the Lees' cabin to do what we do every other day—have a barbecue, play games (the kids), get drunk (the adults)—only this time in much fancier clothes that made us all extremely hot and uncomfortable. But we looked nice for photos, which is what's truly important.

Sebastian and Anna exchanged gifts—he gave her a bottle of perfume, which kind of shocked me. Although not nearly as much as when he turned and handed me a small box in bright red wrapping paper. I protested that I hadn't bought him anything, but he said, "Don't worry about it, Maise. It's from me and Beamer. It's not a big deal, okay?" I busied myself unwrapping it to avoid eye contact with Beamer himself, who was hovering nearby. When I saw it was a Funko Pop figure of the Terminator, my heart nearly burst.

"Thank you. You really shouldn't have," I said to Sebastian. He winked at me. I caught Beamer's hopeful expression behind him, and added, "both of you," before rushing away to help Mum in the kitchen.

Beamer tried to talk to me a couple of times throughout the day, but I somehow found myself very busy. I mean, I just *had* to help Mum and Laura with lunch, and play paddle ball with Kane and Lincoln, and ask Jimmy questions about the cricket for a good half an hour. I even wound up sitting between Eva and Bess at one stage. The situation was that dire.

Eva was doing her over-the-top nice thing, saying, "That dress looks so good on you, Maise," and "Did you make these rum balls? They're yum," and "Bess, Maisie loves movies."

"Everyone loves movies," I said. I picked up two cherries from the platter in front of me and shoved them both in my mouth, trying to limit the expectation of further conversation, but Eva didn't give up that easily.

"Not like *you* love movies."

"What's your favorite?" Bess asked.

"I don't have one," I said around the cherries.

"Seriously?"

"What about *Dirty Dancing*?" Eva said with a smile that made me want to spit the cherry pits straight into her face.

Instead, I did the gracious thing (it being Christmas and all) and spat them out into a napkin, then changed the subject. "I've been meaning to tell you all day, your makeup is so good," I said to Bess, even though I hadn't been meaning to say anything, but desperate times and all. To be fair, her makeup was awesome.

Bess thanked me and then said, "Yours is amazing too. Or more like, ah-*Maise*-ing, am I right?"

I looked at her blankly.

"Get it? Like Maisie...amazing. Ah-*Maise*-ing..."

"Oh, yeah," I said. "Um, thanks." There was an awkward pause.

"Bess is actually a makeup artist," Eva piped up.

"Not professionally or anything," Bess protested. "I'm self-taught. It's just a bit of fun."

"Don't be modest. It's *art*."

For once, I agreed with Eva, but I wasn't about to give her the satisfaction of admitting it out loud. I guess I'm not *that* gracious, even on Christmas. Thankfully, Laura pulled up a chair near us and settled in to eat her pavlova, rescuing me from having to keep the conversation going.

"So," she said between spoonsful. "Eva, tell me—how did you and Bess meet?"

Eva looked over at Bess and smiled affectionately. "Well, I read this personal essay Bess wrote online."

"I'm majoring in journalism," Bess interjected.

"Trying to get as much published as possible before I graduate next year."

"Yeah, so I really liked this piece, and I found her on Twitter and we got chatting. Eventually we met up for coffee, and we just clicked."

The two of them were grinning at each other now, practically sending little cartoon love hearts out of their eyes.

"Ah. Like mother like daughter, eh?" Laura said.

"You mean because Dad's a journalist?" Eva said.

"Well, that. But that's how your mum fell for him. Through his writing."

"Really? I thought they met at a bar."

Laura laughed. "They did. Your mum wasn't interested, but he asked around and figured out which dorm we lived in. He started leaving these little love notes for her in her mailbox. Full of poetry and all sorts of mushy stuff. It won her over in the end."

Mum had appeared at Laura's side by this stage. She rolled her eyes. "He was such a pest." But she had a tiny smile on her face. It looked strained, but it was there.

"Dad? A poet?!" I couldn't believe it.

"No way." Apparently Eva couldn't either.

"Oh yeah. You should have seen the stuff he sent her *after* they started dating," Laura said, standing up and collecting our empty bowls. "It was filthy. What was that one about your—"

"That's enough!" Mum playfully whipped the tea towel she was holding at Laura's butt as she walked toward the trash can. But I wanted to hear more. I got up to follow Laura, then froze when I noticed Beamer was also at the trash can, tossing his own paper bowl away. He caught my eye and took a step toward me.

"Oh, is that the time? You know what, I'm super tired, I'm gonna go have a nap." I took off toward our cabin before anyone could respond.

As you know, I didn't actually have a nap. I ended up writing for a while, spilling my guts about Christmas Eve. That is, until I heard someone sliding open the screen door. Then there was a knock at my bedroom door.

"Maisie? Can I come in?"

I contemplated not answering, except knowing Beamer, he'd probably just keep knocking. I even considered jumping through the tiny window, but visions of getting stuck like some sort of bad slapstick comedy (or, worse, a horror movie) stopped me.

"Hey," he said when I opened the door.

"What do you want?"

"I, uh..." He cleared his throat and stepped into the room. "I thought maybe we should talk? About... um...last night?"

"What's there to talk about? We were drunk, we were there, no big deal. You're off the hook."

About five different emotions played across his face, but I couldn't quite place any of them. He sighed.

"Maisie..." He opened and closed his mouth a few times, as if he kept changing his mind about what he wanted to say. For a brief moment I flashed back to the night before, to that mouth on mine, but I quickly pushed the thought away

"Beamer, what are you doing here? Spit it out or get out," I snapped.

He frowned. "What's your problem?"

"My problem? *My* problem?! Among other things, you dared me to kiss you and then when I did—"

"I never thought you'd actually do it." His voice was raised slightly.

"Well, I'm sorry," I said, sarcasm dripping from my words.

"No, that's not what I meant—I meant...I don't know what I meant." He sat down on the bed, looking frustrated.

I crossed my arms, still standing. "Whatever, it's fine, like I said."

We were interrupted by my phone vibrating. It was Dad calling.

"Hey Dad, what's up? Is everything okay?"

"Eminem, hey! Yeah, everything's great, still at your grandma's. How was lunch?"

"It was alright. I had to peel my own prawns."

He chuckled. "Sorry I couldn't be there. Hey, I was

just ringing to see if your mum's around? Her phone is dead, I think. I'm not getting through. I didn't get a chance to talk to her this morning."

"Oh...I'm not with Mum right now. I'll go get her."

"That's alright, Em, I'll try again later. Love you." He hung up without waiting for my response. My heart sank, and I sank down on the bed with it. Tears stung my eyes. Were my parents ever going to talk to each other again?

"Are you okay?" Beamer said quietly.

I breathed out heavily and shook my head. "Why do I keep crying in front of you?" My voice was shaky. I was trying really hard not to sob.

"I have that effect on women," he said. I snorted.

"It's my dad," I explained. "It's just...I wish he were here, is all. Things are weird right now. With my parents, I mean. I don't know. It...it doesn't feel right, being here without him. Like it's not Christmas. It's silly, I guess."

"Nah." Beamer inched slightly closer to me. "You know, I almost didn't come this year. I've always felt bad about leaving my gran at Christmas, but she insists I come every time. She jokes that it's a holiday for her too." He chuckled softly. "But Cal, my sister, she's living in London now and she couldn't make it back, and my gran...she's not doing that great—not that she'd ever admit it. But she said she wouldn't forgive me if I didn't come. That she'd prefer to know I was having fun and, anyway, she'd get sick of the sight of my ugly mug if she had to put up with it every day." I smiled at the affection on his face. "I still feel guilty, though."

"She wouldn't say those things if they weren't true, right?"

He sniffed. "I mean, she always puts us first. I worry about what she really wants, what she really needs deep down, you know?" He stood up and paced the room. "Maybe I shouldn't have come."

"Have you spoken to her today?"

"Yeah," he said, smiling. "She was getting pissed with her mates."

"See! She's having a great time without you."

He laughed at that. After a moment, he took a step toward me, then seemed to think better of it and turned away, before finally turning around again and sitting down next to me with such force he bounced a little on the bed. His next words came out in a rush: "Hey, so, I was thinkin', about last night? Like, maybe we should try that again?"

It took me a minute to process what he had said. And when I did—

"What?!"

He swallowed and took a breath, leaning back to rest on his elbow. "Well, with Seb and Anna..." He glanced at me and then quickly looked away. "I just mean, y'know, why not? We've got all this free time, and we can't spend *all* of it watching The Rock— although I personally could, y'know, but um, it was fun. Last night, I mean. It was really fun. Why not have some more fun?"

"You mean, like...a friends with benefits kinda thing? Except without the friends bit?"

He sat up, scratching his chin. "Ha. Uh, yeah, I guess. I mean, if you wanted to."

"Why? Like, why me?"

"I mean..." He looked around. Right. Because there was no one else around.

"And what kind of benefits?"

He looked at me and tilted his head, a slow smile spreading on his face. "Any kind you want, Maisie Martin."

And something in the way he said that made me want to kiss him again. There was a warm feeling deep in my stomach, a hunger I hadn't felt before. At least not around Beamer.

So for the second time in as many days, I reached out to grasp his neck, and brought my lips to his.

When we broke apart, I said, "Don't think this means we're friends now."

He grinned, and with his usual airy voice, said, "Definitely not, Maisie Martin."

* * *

Leila's verdict on all this?
1. He's into me.
2. Am I sure I'm not into him?
3. She is so here for all of it.
I told Leila:
1. No.
2. Yes (I'm sure). No (I'm not).
3. Same, to be honest.

Look, it's weird. It's *Beamer*. But as long as I don't think too hard about it...why not have some fun, like he said?

Especially when I've got other things to worry about. Like my parents. Like the fact that I've decided to stand in front of a bunch of people and be judged on the way I look in less than two weeks.

Honestly, I really do question my own judgment sometimes.

* * *

Anna pounced on me as soon as I got home from shopping with Leila. "Maise, thank god, save me. They've had cricket on *all day* and I'm bored out of my brain. Let's do something fun tonight."

Beamer sidled up next to her. "Aren't we doing *Central Intelligence* tonight?"

Anna rolled her eyes. "Ugh, seriously?"

"Nah, we don't have to," I said, glancing at Beamer and trying to ignore the way he slapped his hand to his chest and pulled a face of mock heartbreak.

Suddenly Sebastian was there, wrapping his arms around Anna from behind and nuzzling her neck. The smoothie I'd had earlier threatened to make a reappearance.

Mum came out of her bedroom and breezed through the lounge room, talking as she walked toward the door. "Maisie, there you are—how was your day—great—we're going to the movies to see that new Nicholas Sparks—are you sure you don't want to come—fine—Jimmy's making dinner for the twins if you want to go over there or there's some frozen pizzas in the freezer—just don't burn the place down." And she was gone.

I turned to the others, about to kick Sebastian and

150

Beamer out so Anna and I could have the place to ourselves, when she said, "You know, frozen pizza and a terrible movie sounds really good, actually."

I was puzzled by Anna's change of heart, until about halfway through the movie. We'd already scoffed down the plastic-cheese-on-cardboard that was the frozen pizza, and she and Sebastian got up and disappeared into the bedroom Anna and I share, closing the door behind them.

There was that delightful queasy feeling back again. I sighed and got up, walking over to the kitchenette to refill my drink.

"You want anything?" I said to Beamer over my shoulder.

"Yeah, I do," he said. I grabbed his cup from him and our fingers brushed. I was suddenly very aware that we were alone together. In a darkened room. Oh god. Were we supposed to make out? How exactly did this work? Did he want to? Did *I* want to?

All these questions were racing through my head as I settled back on the lounge, sitting as far away from him as possible. I tucked my legs up next to me, holding a cushion to my stomach and staring at the screen. The hairs on my neck prickled as I sensed Beamer watching me. I looked over at him just in time to see him quickly turn his head away. I let myself gaze at him for a moment. His hair was messy but seemed really soft. I had the sudden urge to run my fingers through it. I kept my hand very firmly at my side and looked back at the screen, taking a huge gulp of my drink.

A few minutes later, I felt him staring at me again. I turned my head and again he looked away, but this time he laughed, self-conscious. He bit his lip and looked back over at me. Our eyes locked. Between us and around us, the room buzzed, as though the air was charged with electricity. The hairs on my arms were standing on end and part of me wouldn't have been surprised if the hair on my head spontaneously defied gravity too. The rest of me was totally focused on Beamer, though. He licked his lips and looked at mine. My heart was thumping in my chest.

Slowly, taking great care with all his movements, like he was afraid he'd startle me if he moved too quickly, he slid closer. When there was little space left between us, he paused, looking into my eyes. I swallowed hard. He reached up to cup my face, his thumb grazing my cheek.

Finally, after what felt like an excruciating amount of time, he closed the distance between our lips. The kiss started off slow and gentle and then became more urgent. I let my hands do what they wanted to and ran them through his hair, grasping handfuls, willing him closer to me. It wasn't enough.

Without breaking the kiss, I pushed him back against the lounge, straddling him. He made an appreciative noise and my insides melted. The cushion that had been on my lap was still between us, and he tugged it away so our bodies were even closer. I inwardly cringed as his hands found the soft flesh of my stomach. I pulled back, breathing heavily. Our faces were still close. He had a hazy look in his eyes as he leaned in toward me, his mouth open and half smiling. He kissed a trail from my neck up to my mouth. I closed my eyes, willing my self-consciousness away, willing myself to get lost in his kisses. In his touch. In his—okay, that's all you're getting, DJ, you dirty perv.

I'll give you a little spoiler: there was no significant under-the-clothes action. When I heard the bedroom door open I sprung off Beamer, knocking over my drink, which was on the floor by his feet. I reached for the paper towel, left out from when we were eating pizza earlier, and mopped it up without looking up. My face felt like it was on fire. Beamer chuckled, and I glanced up in time to see Sebastian settling back on the lounge next to him. Anna was nowhere to be seen, but I heard the water running in the bathroom. Judging by the pretty neutral look on Sebastian's face, I was guessing he hadn't seen anything. I was hoping, at least.

"This still going?" he said.

Beamer just grunted.

"Need a hand, Maise?" Sebastian asked.

"Nah, I'm good," I said, straightening up and noticing that Beamer's hair was sticking up all over the place, worse than usual. Oh god.

I dumped the sodden paper towel in the trash and boiled the pot to make a cup of tea, not really knowing what to do with myself. Anna finally came out of the bathroom and sat down on the floor in front of Sebastian, leaning her head into his knee.

"This still going?" she said, and Sebastian laughed.

Beamer, sounding like his normal self, said, "Maisie Martin, get your butt back here, you're missing the best part."

I took a deep breath and returned to sit with them, but to be honest I didn't really take in much of the movie.

After the boys left, I got a message from Beamer. *Was that your attempt to sabotage me in this competition, Maisie Martin? I expect a fair score. In fact, I expect bonus points for the live entertainment.*

As we exchanged messages back and forth, I felt

myself grinning. Then Leila's voice ran through my head. *"He's so into you! And you're into him too, aren't you? You like him?!"* I looked down at the message I was in the middle of composing. What had got into me? I deleted my words without hitting send and put down the phone.

Wednesday, 27 December

2 things I discovered today:

1. Dad's not answering his phone. Again. And it's not just me he's avoiding.

Evidence: Jimmy asked me today if I'd been able to reach Dad, because he wasn't answering Jimmy's texts. I hadn't tried to call him since I spoke to him on Christmas Day, but when I did today it just went straight to voicemail. I called his work number instead, but the line was busy. When I told Jimmy this at dinner, he said, "Don't worry, I'm sure he's just working hard." From the other end of the table, Mum said, "Who wants more wine?"

2. In happier news, apparently I'm good at more than just Wookiee impressions.

Evidence: Leila informs me I am also skilled at other impressions. What an accomplishment!

* * *

Back to the beach this morning. I didn't bother putting on a swimsuit (either the old or the new ones Eva and Bess gave me for Christmas, which are actually really nice—a black bikini embroidered with pink flowers; I haven't dared try it on yet). I didn't plan on staying long. I had to go to Leila's so she could work on my dress.

Guess who we ran into at the beach? Eva and Bess. They were both in bikinis. I tried not to stare.

I mean...Bess is fatter than me. Yet there she was, on the beach, in a bikini (this cute blue-and-white-striped number with frills), like it was nothing.

And there was Eva, standing next to her, beaming, like at any other time she wouldn't have been whispering, *"Gee, that girl's got a lot of* guts," and snickering at her own cleverness and superiority.

I don't know what her game is, but I'm not sure I like it.

As for Bess, well, she did have a lot of guts. I wanted to ask her how she got them, and how I could get some, but I think we're probably not yet at that stage of our relationship where I can be like, "Hey, Bess, how do you dare have the confidence to appear in public like that, since you're so FAT and all?" Somehow there doesn't seem to be a way to ask that question without sounding really weird and insulting.

Anyway, I hightailed it out of there soon after the two of them made their appearance, because Eva was acting all excited to see us and I couldn't handle another second of her fakery. At least my plans with Leila gave me a legit excuse, not that I needed one. Anna asked if I wanted her to come too, but I could tell her heart wasn't in it, so I left her chilling with Sebastian and Beamer on the beach (the latter said, "See ya later," and I swear he put extra meaning into it that I hope no one else noticed).

* * *

In addition to an evening gown, Leila has promised to make me a *fabulous* cover-up for the swimwear section of the pageant so I don't feel so self-conscious—"It'll basically be a dress!"—which is great except just the thought of standing on stage, even fully clothed, still makes me feel naked.

"Why am I doing this again?" I moaned to Leila, who was bent over her sketchpad, her tongue poking out of the side of her mouth as she concentrated.

She looked up at me. "Because you want to. Because it will be fun. Because you will feel amazing," she said. "Stop questioning it, okay? I'm serious, I don't want to hear another 'Why did I do this?' from you. If you're in, you're in, and that means only positivity from here on out."

"Yes, boss," I said, trying not to sound as worried as I felt.

"Oh my god, you know what we should do?" Leila held up her pencil next to her head like she'd just had a brilliant idea. "Stream a whole bunch of beauty pageant movies and have a marathon. I bet making fun of them will totally get you in the mood."

I smiled. "Ooh, baby, I love it when you talk dirty to me."

She laughed and threw her pencil at me.

I threw a cushion at her, which she expertly caught.

"Let's do it Friday night," she suggested. "We can go to Jo's—we always do movie nights at hers."

"She won't mind?"

"No way! Just be prepared for her to rant about how sexist the movies are. It's part of her charm." She pulled out her phone and started typing. A few minutes later she said, "Done. The others are in too."

We talked about our plans for New Year's (there's a carnival on the foreshore that everyone's going to) and then got on to the subject of the dreaded year ahead (and beyond).

"Ugh, I just want the year to be over," Leila said. She was leaning over her desk, sketching again. "I wanted to leave school in Year 10 and do a design course full-time, but my parents freaked. I had to beg them to let me do this fashion course on top of my regular school work."

"At least you know what you want to do. I have no idea." I paced the room, tossing a pompom from one hand to the other. "I can't even figure out a talent for this ridiculous beauty pageant! How am I going to find something that could sustain a whole career?"

"Well, what are you good at?"

I snorted. "Not much."

She glanced up at me, shaking her head. "We seriously need to work on your self-esteem."

I sighed and flopped down on her bed. She was rattling off a list of possible talents, each more ridiculous than the last ("You could learn that balancing plates trick!") when there was a knock on the door. I sat up, expecting it to be one of Leila's parents or brothers, and got a shock when Beamer walked in.

"What are you doing here?!" I squeaked at the same time as Leila said, "Heeey!" and got up to give him a hug.

"Thought I'd come see where the magic happens," he said, looking around. Leila sat back down, telling him to make himself at home. He started walking around her room, picking things up and examining them before putting them back down. "There's only so much of the lovebirds I can take," he said as he manhandled Leila's dress form.

"We were just talking about Maisie's talent for the pageant," Leila said.

"Oh yeah? I thought you'd decided on your Chewbacca impression," Beamer said with a smirk. He picked up a rock that had two googly eyes stuck on it and gave Leila a questioning look.

"Would you stop touching everything? It's rude," I said.

"It's alright, I don't mind," Leila said, smiling. "That's Rocky. Jo made him for me when we were seven. He knows all my secrets."

"Ah, of course. Sorry, Rocky, didn't mean to disturb you." Beamer put the rock back on the dresser and sat near me on the bed.

I stood up and cleared a space on Leila's orange chair. Beamer rolled his eyes.

"Wait. Beamer, you're a genius," Leila said.

"I am?"

"He is?"

"Yes! Babe, your talent!"

"A Chewbacca impression?" I screwed up my face.

"Not just that. I've seen you do a bunch of impressions! They're hilarious. Your Hermione Granger at the party the other night had everyone in stitches."

"I can't just stand on stage and do impressions for two minutes."

"Why the hell not?"

"It's not really a talent. It's silly."

"Oh my god, stop. It's brilliant! Here, I'll prove it to you. Watch my Hermione." She pursed her lips and said in her normal voice, "'It's Leviosa, not Leviosa.'"

"'It's LeviOsa, not LevioSA,'" I corrected, in a pretty close imitation of Emma Watson (if I do say so myself).

"See? That's perfect! Don't you think, Beamer?"

He looked at me thoughtfully.

I was expecting a smart-arse comment, so I was pretty surprised when he said, "Why don't you do that dance you wanted to do? The *Dirty Dancing* one?"

I frowned. "How do you know about that?"

He shrugged. "Don't dodge the question."

"Says the person dodging my question," I retorted.

He just raised his eyebrows, waiting.

I sighed. "Well, for starters, it's kind of a two-person routine."

"Aren't you allowed, like, an assistant or something?"

"And how do you know *that*?"

"I've watched *Toddlers and Tiaras*," he said, like it was the most normal thing in the world. "What? My gran loves it."

"Yeah, well, I'm not a toddler."

"Wait, I've seen people do dances with partners before," Leila chimed in. "You could totally do it!"

I shook my head. "I can't dance."

Beamer started to say something, but I spoke over the top of him. "You know what? Impressions are a great idea. I can do that. Totally." And I launched into my best Russell Crowe from *Gladiator*: "'Are you not entertained?!'"

* * *

Later, as Beamer and I were huddled in a sand dune after leaving Leila's, spending some quality time not talking, he broke away from me and ruined it by talking.

"Hey, uh, can I ask you something?"

"No," I said, leaning in to kiss him again.

He put a hand to my face to stop me, his fingers sliding across my cheek before tucking my hair behind my ear. "Why don't you wanna do that dance?"

I pulled away from him, turning to face the ocean. "I really can't dance."

"Yes, you can."

"No, I can't."

"Yes, you can. I've seen you. You—"

"That was a long time ago," I said, cutting him off.

"I don't see how that—"

"You don't get it."

"Try me."

I let out a frustrated sigh, looking down at my hands as I ran them through the cool sand. "Girls like me...we're not made for dancing."

"What?"

"It's like—you know that bit in *Dirty Dancing*, where Johnny says, 'Nobody puts Baby in a corner'?" I glanced at him and he opened his mouth, but I didn't give him a chance to answer. "It's so romantic, right? Like, he plucks her out of the corner and puts a spotlight on her because he *sees* her, and he demands that everyone else see her, too. And he lifts her up the way she deserves to be lifted up. And—well, meanwhile, girls like me...we stay in the corner."

Beamer didn't say anything, and when I glanced at him he seemed thoughtful, rubbing his thumb across his lips. Finally, he said, "That's bullshit."

"Excuse me?!"

"Bull. Shit. If you wanna dance, *dance*."

I shook my head. "I told you—"

"I know, I know, you can't. But when was the last time you even tried?"

"I can't remember," I lied.

"Well, come on then. Have a go." He got up, dusted sand off his butt and held his hand out to me.

"What, now? Here?!"

"Now. Here." He waved his outstretched hand impatiently.

"What is it with you and dancing on beaches?"

"It's as good a place as any." He looked around. "Come on, there's no one here."

"We'd better get back." I got up and, ignoring his hand, walked past him. "We don't want anyone getting suspicious. They can*not* know about...whatever this is."

"Yeah. We wouldn't want that," he said, trailing after me.

* * *

At dinner, Beamer asked the twins if they wanted to join us to watch *Last Action Hero*, our final Schwarzenegger (it was a tough choice, but I went with it for the pure meta joy of it all). Jimmy piped up that he loved that movie, which had a domino effect, and we ended up with pretty much everyone crowded around the TV to watch it. Only Eva and Bess were missing because they'd gone on a date. Everyone kept talking over the top of the movie, and laughing in the wrong spots. At one point Mum said, "We better be quiet, Maisie will get in a mood." Which, of course, put me in a mood.

I got out my phone and messaged Beamer: *WTF?? Is this *your* attempt to sabotage *me* now?*

He was sitting on the floor across the room from me, and I saw him look at his phone. He rolled his eyes and started typing.

Nah. I just didn't want anyone getting suspicious. He ended with a winking face emoji and turned his own face to the TV without once looking at me.

Thursday, 28 December

3 things I discovered today:

1. There are way more than seven layers of hell. There has to be. Because I discovered, like, the hundredth today. I was IN IT.

Evidence: Not only did I go shopping, but I did it with the four horsemen of the apocalypse. Well, that's kinda unfair on Bess and Anna, I suppose, but two horsemen (or, rather, horsewomen) doesn't quite have the same ring to it. What I'm trying to say is, Mum and Eva are the apocalyptic horsepeople in question in this tortured metaphor, okay?

2. My sister is just full of surprises.

Evidence: She let something out today that she's been keeping from everyone, and it was NUCLEAR.

3. I don't hate everything about myself.

Evidence: Some quality self-examination time (not in *that* way—get your mind out of the gutter).

* * *

What. A. Day. I'll go back to the start.

I've been missing Anna. Mum was right (never tell her I said that); things have been weird and I want to get *us* back. That's why I suggested we do something together at breakfast.

"Hey, that's a great idea, why don't we all have a girlie day?" Mum said before Anna could answer. "We can go shopping and get mani-pedis. Maisie, is there anything you need for the pageant? You really should be—"

"No, it's fine, Mum, I told you."

"I just don't know if it's a good idea to get a student to make your gown. Wouldn't you rather put the money toward something professional?"

We'd been through this already. A few times. I stared down at the fruit salad in my bowl without saying anything.

"I don't understand why you won't let Eva and me help you with this. We've done it all before, you know, and we had so much fun. This could be something we do together. We don't do anything together anymore."

We've never done anything together, I wanted to say, but I bit my tongue. It was too early for an argument.

Next to me, Anna said quietly, "Didn't you say you needed shoes, Maise?"

Mum went in for the kill. "Oh, I know the perfect place. I'll call Eva." She got up and raced inside before I could get a word out, even though her mobile was in her hand the whole time.

I shot Anna a look.

"Sorry," she said. "I just thought—your mum is so keen to do this for you. It's nice."

I shook my head. "Don't you know? It's not for me. It's never for me. It's for her. So she can control everything. So I don't damage her perfect image any more than I already have."

From inside, Mum called out, "We're picking Eva and Bess up in ten. Get a move on, girls."

I stood up, the chair legs scraping against the concrete harshly as I did so.

"Let's get this over with," I muttered.

* * *

You know, for a brief, fleeting moment, as the five of us sat around a table in a coffee shop and chatted, I actually thought maybe it wouldn't be so bad.

Then Mum started talking about how many calories were in everything, and how she couldn't afford to put on any more weight, and I could feel the mercury levels rising on my Urge-To-Scream-ometer.

"Ah, you only get one body, you might as well enjoy it," Bess said with a smile as Mum was looking longingly at a piece of chocolate cake.

"Yes, exactly," Mum said. And didn't order the cake.

At the shoe store, Mum kept on picking up impossibly high heels, even though I very clearly couldn't walk in them.

"You'll just have to practice, Maisie—you've got over a week! Eva and I will help you." She smiled at Eva.

"Yeah, totally—we'll do that book-balancing thing," Eva said with a slightly evil grin.

I groaned.

"What about these?" Bess said, picking up a pair of black strappy sandals.

I tried them on. They were *perfect*. Sure, they weren't the flashiest, but they were way more comfortable than any of the others I'd tried.

Mum screwed up her nose. "You know it's called a beauty pageant, not a comfort pageant, right?" She cracked up laughing at her own joke.

"Leila said to go for something simple," I argued.

"I'm not a fan, Maise," Anna piped up. "I think you can do better."

I sighed and put the shoes back. We ended up buying a pair of wedges that I don't think *any* of us really liked, but at least I could (almost) walk in them.

I'm not even going to go into the torture that was my mother dragging us all around Target to find the perfect pair of Spanx for me, except to say that when I moaned she snapped, "Well, I don't know why you entered the pageant if you're not even going to bother trying."

By the time we hit the food court for lunch, everyone seemed rather frazzled, as my grandma would say. I ordered a salad, even though I was really craving McDonald's. I just didn't have the energy to deal with a double-whammy lecture from Eva and Mum about my eating habits.

But maybe I shouldn't have worried. Because the weirdest thing happened. Mum turned on *Eva*.

Apparently Eva has developed a late-stage rebellious streak.

Mum was asking her about her dance course and

what she's going to be doing next year, and Eva was giving her really short, vague answers. She kept glancing at Bess, who was raising her eyebrows and looking pointedly at Mum.

"Alright, what's going on?" Mum said, dropping her fork on the table and clasping her hands together in front of her in the way she does when she's pissed off.

"Nothing," Eva said, but she couldn't meet Mum's eyes. Which was probably a good thing, because Mum was sending one of her most cutting death stares Eva's way.

"Why don't you just tell her?" Bess said quietly, and Eva sent a death stare of her own. (They run in the family. Hey, maybe that should be my talent for the beauty pageant: terrify the audience with a single glare.)

"Tell me what?" Mum said. She was all out of patience; I could tell by the way her mouth had tightened so much it had begun to resemble a dog's bum hole.

Eva sighed. "Let's just talk about it when we get home, alright? In private."

Mum looked at her for a second, probably weighing up just how far she could push it right then, and made her decision. "Alright, let's go." She got up and headed straight for the parking lot without looking back.

And so ended the shopping trip from the hundredth layer of hell.

* * *

DJ, you are not going to believe what Eva's big secret was. *I* can barely believe it.

SHE WANTS TO CHANGE DEGREES. SHE WANTS TO QUIT DANCING. SHE DOESN'T LOVE IT ANYMORE. SHE DOESN'T SEE THE POINT.

Her whole life, she's dedicated herself to this one pursuit—to performing, to being professional, to being perfect—and now, all of a sudden, she wants to chuck it all in.

You should have heard Mum ranting. She was mad enough when I quit dancing, and that was just because of what she called my "attitude" and subsequent activity levels (or lack thereof). With Eva, it's so much worse. This was supposed to be her career. Her life. And oh, Mum let her know it: "After everything we've sacrificed—after all your hard work—you haven't thought this through—I can't believe—what has got into you—" It went on and on. She even phoned Dad, and he picked up. Yep, incredibly, Eva actually got Mum to speak to him again—although really all Mum was doing was screaming at him about "your daughter!" as though she'd somehow forgotten she was also responsible for the conception, birth, and raising of my sister.

I'd had enough by this point. I grabbed Anna and we snuck out the door. We walked down the beach, not saying much. I guess we were both lost in our own thoughts. Do you want to know what mine were, DJ? I'd never admit this out loud, not to anyone—not even to Anna. But a small part of me was kind of thrilled that, for once, the golden child was the disappointment. For once, the shine had worn off.

Another part of me was hurt. Mum talked about what she and Dad—what Eva—had sacrificed, and how it had all been for nothing. But what about what I'd sacrificed? What about how I had *been* the sacrifice?

It wasn't just how Eva's dancing had always taken priority in our family, and how all of Mum's spare time had gone into supporting her. It was Eva and everything she'd said and done to let me know I was less important than this thing in her life—that I wasn't worthy of her dancing. Now that thing was worthless, where did that leave me?

But you know what else, DJ? There were other parts of me that felt very different. Parts that kind of took me by surprise, after everything that's happened.

Like the part of me that was in awe of my sister. For what it must have taken her to make this choice and go through with it. For sticking to her guns, standing up to Mum, for making a whole new sacrifice by tossing aside her role as the perfect daughter, the perfect dancer, the perfect everything.

And that last part? That last part of me was really worried about my big sister.

* * *

After we'd been walking for awhile, Anna asked if I was okay.

"Me? I'm fine. Why wouldn't I be?"

"That was pretty intense back there," she said.

"You know what my family's like," I said. I didn't particularly want to go into the conflicting feelings crashing around inside of me. So I said, "What do you want to do tonight?" And the subject was dropped.

We decided to go bowling with the boys in town, because staying within a one-mile radius of the war zone that was Mum and Eva seemed like a terrible idea.

We were halfway through our second game (I was winning—I am the strike queen) when Anna and Sebastian went to get drinks and didn't come back.

They'd been all handsy and giggly all night. Beamer and I...hadn't. He was back to his usual annoying self, ribbing me about my technique, boasting about his own. When I beat him round after round he just grinned and said, "It's all part of the plan." Uh-huh.

"Should I go find them?" I said, after fifteen minutes had gone by and there was no sign of Anna and Sebastian. Beamer gave me a look.

"Guess they forfeit, then," I said, getting up to take Anna's turn for her. I faced away from the lane, bent over and rolled the ball between my legs. It hit the pins in the middle, creating a split.

"Shot!" Beamer cried, laughing.

For my next go I lifted my right leg across my body and swung the ball under it, completely missing all the remaining pins.

"Beat that," I said. Beamer grinned and cracked his neck and his knuckles before reaching for his ball. He acted like it was as heavy as a boulder, bending his back and dangling the ball between his legs, using both hands to hold it. He hobbled up to the line like that, then bent over, placing the ball gently on the lane.

"Stop checking out my butt," he called, wiggling it in the air.

I laughed and called out, "You wish!" even though that's exactly what I'd been doing.

He gave the ball a push and straightened up with a hop, backing up to stand by me as we watched the ball move at an achingly slow pace down the lane. It finally stopped about three feet from the actual pins. We had to get the guy behind the counter to retrieve it.

"Alright, no more slow balls," I said, but we were both cracking up. We spent the rest of the game taking it in turns to bowl as fast as we could, with as many different ridiculous poses as we could think of. A couple of times we both bowled at the same time, the balls ricocheting off each other, until one got stuck against the pin-retriever machine thingy (I'm sure they have an actual name, but I don't know it) and the guy who'd helped us earlier threatened to kick us out.

There was still no sign of Anna and Sebastian, so Beamer and I headed to the arcade, unable to stop giggling. I grabbed Beamer's hand and pulled him into the old-fashioned photo booth.

As the first flash went off, we looked at each other, breathless and smiling.

As the second snapped, he leaned in closer so our faces were nearly touching.

As the third went off, he brought his lips to mine.

And as the fourth clicked, I looked at the camera

in surprise as he whispered in my ear, "You're so beautiful."

If this were a montage in a movie, it would have been all romantic and cute. It would have been with the dreamy leading guy and the beautiful leading girl, not the smart-arse best friend and the chubby sidekick. But Anna and Sebastian were off making out somewhere in the dark—probably next to the dumpster, let's be real. Because life is not a movie.

So I rolled my eyes, pushed Beamer out of the booth, and proceeded to kick his butt at air hockey. But I left the bowling alley with that strip of photos burning a hole in my back pocket.

* * *

When we got home, I jumped in the shower. After I dried myself, I wiped the steam off the long mirror attached to the back of the bathroom door.

I was thinking about Beamer and those three whispered words, "You're so beautiful." He probably didn't mean it. Did he?

As I considered my reflection, trying to see some kind of beauty, and failing as I always do, something Eva had screamed at Mum when they were at their battle stations earlier floated back to me. Mum had been yelling "Why?" a lot, and it was like something in Eva snapped, and she burst out with, "I got tired of looking in the mirror all the time and hating what I saw."

Tired. That's exactly how I felt. Tired—and sad. Because if someone like *Eva* feels like that—well, what hope do I have?

Then I thought of Bess. About how she had said you only have one body, so you might as well enjoy it. She was talking about eating cake. But also, I think, about so much more. I've noticed something in the past few days. She's really comfortable in her own skin. Confident, even. It's amazing.

I can't remember the last time I felt that way. Comfortable inside my skin. Can you imagine that, DJ? Humor me for a second, and pretend you're not an inanimate object but a real human being with real human feelings.

Imagine having a body that you're always uncomfortable in. *Always.* That moves when you want it to be still, and makes you want to be still even when you long to move. That doesn't look how you want it to look or feel how you want it to feel.

Imagine seeing those things in your own reflection.

Imagine having a body that people stare at wherever you go. Pass silent judgment on. Pierce your skin and get at your soul with their wide eyes. With their raised eyebrows. With their twisted mouths.

Imagine seeing that look on the face of your own mother.

Imagine having a body that people feel they can comment on. Pass loud judgment on. Pierce your skin and get at your soul with their cruel words. Their taunts. Even their concern, which is really just another way of saying you're not good enough.

Imagine hearing those words from your own sister.

Imagine having a body that is never seen in the movies you love, or the TV shows you watch, except when it's being mocked. Treated as a horror, a freak show, something to be laughed at.

Imagine hearing that laughter from your own father.

Imagine having a body that is to be feared. That turns you into a living cautionary tale, the "before" that people want to get away from, the "after" they desperately want to avoid. That's described in words thin people use to put themselves down, to say they feel awful—they can't go out, they're having a "fat" day, as though it's a viral infection they need to ride out.

Imagine hearing those words from your best friend.

Can you feel it yet, DJ? Can you feel how unrelentingly exhausting it is? Can you feel the little holes opening up in your soul, an emptiness inside of you that can't be filled?

I saw this quote on Instagram one time, this thing about how nobody can really love you until you love yourself. But how can you love yourself when even the people who are supposed to love you no matter what can't accept who you are?

I'm tired of it. I'm so fucking tired of it.

So I stood there tonight, in front of the mirror. And I cried. And I wiped my tears away, and I looked at myself. Truly *looked* at myself for the first time in a long time. And I counted the things I like about my body. It went like this:

1. My eyes.
2. My eyebrows.
3. My ears.
4. My hair.
5. My fingernails.
6. My boobs.
7. My forearms.

That's it. Seven things. Just seven things.

But you know what, DJ? It's better than nothing.

And you know what else? Next time, maybe it'll be eight.

You've got to start somewhere, right? And here's the thing: I might not love my body right now. But I'm sure as hell done with feeling ashamed of it.

Friday, 29 December

4 things I discovered today:

1. My dress for the pageant is NEARLY ready.

Evidence: Leila. Unfortunately I don't have primary evidence because she won't let me see it until it's DONE. Which she promises will be very soon.

2. Being interviewed is harder than it looks.

Evidence: A journalist from the lifestyle section of the local news site interviewed me today for a piece she's running about the pageant on Sunday. Chirpy Janice, who was the one who informed me I'd been accepted, rang me this morning to set it up. I said yes without really thinking, and then promptly started shitting myself. (Like I actually had to run to the toilet a few times. Sorry if that's too much information, DJ.)

3. Dad is officially a more useless parent than my mother.

Evidence: When I texted him, you know, the EXPERT at interviews, for advice, all he wrote back was: *You'll do great, Eminem! How's your mother?* At least he wrote back, I guess.

4. I think we might have accidentally entered into a parallel dimension without realizing it. Maybe it was those dodgy burritos we had the other night.

Evidence: See point 3, and also the fact that Mum is really pissed with Eva...and really happy with me???

* * *

Mum was in a foul mood this morning. The climate in the cabin was so frosty, it was like Elsa had come to stay. Mum had barely thawed when she came back from her pamper session with Laura at the spa. ("I'll sort her out," Laura had whispered to me as she whisked Mum out the door. She gave me a helpless shrug behind Mum's back when they returned.)

But you know what snapped her out of it? ME (?!??!??!!).

"What's going on?" Mum said when she saw Anna

and me surrounded by piles of my clothes and an air of despair. I was supposed to be meeting Sarah, the journalist who wanted to interview me, in fifteen minutes, and I had no idea what to wear. When I told Mum what was happening, she shrieked. Like, ear-bursting excitement.

"Oh my gosh, Missy-May! You must be a favorite if they're nominating you for press." She looked me up and down. "Oh. You're not wearing that, are you?"

After a flurry of "helpful" suggestions from Mum, encouragement from Laura, and meaningful looks from Anna, I was finally out the door in jeans and a flowing blue top. Mum tried to come with me, but I grabbed Anna's hand and shot out of there before she could even ask where we were going.

We met Sarah on the path near the main beach. She was stunning, with tanned skin, perfect eyebrows, and a smile that was whiter and straighter than all the leading men in Hollywood. She had a camera guy with her and held a microphone with the news site's logo on it up to my face. I felt Very Important.

Sarah asked me questions about myself and how much pageant experience I'd had, and I heard Mum's voice in my head telling me: *Speak naturally but not too fast, and smile, but not too much. Be bright, Missy, let her see your shine!* So I smiled and said perkily, "This will be my first pageant, but it runs in the family."

Her ears pricked up at that (metaphorically—her literal ears were hidden under her voluminous dark hair, but they might have pricked up, who knows). Soon I was answering questions about Eva, and I dug deep to muster way more enthusiasm than I felt. I was all, *"Yes! Eva's been helping me prepare and giving me great advice! Oh, you know, the usual: smile big, wave like the queen, strut like Beyoncé. Hahaha—yeah she's just great. Oh no, Mum isn't a stage mum at all. She is supportive of whatever we want to do!"*

Gag me with a spoon.

"How did you feel when you found out you were in the competition?" Sarah asked.

"I was surprised, to be honest."

"Why were you surprised?"

Gulp. "Well, when I entered, I never thought I'd actually get through." Smile!

"And why was that?"

Deep breath, don't look down, look up! Smile! "It's just such an honor to be here." Oscar nominees, eat your heart out.

"But why did you enter if you didn't think you'd get in?"

"Well, you never know if you don't try I guess, ha ha!"

"Was there anything in particular you were concerned about?"

Smile. Smile. Smile.

"Was your body shape something you were worried about?"

Am I still smiling? I don't think I'm still smiling. I don't know what my mouth is doing. Unclench those teeth. Smile! Gulp.

"Um, a little, yeah, I guess." Not smiling.

"So how did it feel when you got in?"

"Um...surprising, like I said."

"But how did you *feel*?"

Deep breath. Perk up. "Great! Just great! So excited! It's going to be great!" Grin, grin, grin.

Sarah finally changed the subject to how I was preparing for the pageant and wrapped up not long after. Then the camera guy got me to walk along the beach and stare out at the ocean. I felt Very Silly.

After they'd left and Anna and I were walking up the beach, she told me I'd done really well.

"I dunno, that felt...weird?"

"She was a little pushy, wasn't she? But you were awesome. How exciting, Maise, I'm so proud of you!" She put her arm around me as we walked and I actually began to let myself feel excited.

Tonight was movie night at Jo's, and it was a lot of fun. We ate way too much and laughed even more. By the time I got home, my cheeks were sore from smiling. Genuine smiles this time, not the forced grimaces from earlier in the day. And when I looked in the mirror, I added to the list of things I like:

1. My eyes.
2. My eyebrows.
3. My ears.
4. My hair.
5. My fingernails.
6. My boobs.
7. My forearms.
8. My smile.

Saturday, 30 December

3 things I discovered today:

1. Apparently there are sporting events I will voluntarily attend.

Evidence: I went—willingly—with Leila and co. to watch Kieron play cricket. CRICKET. But you know what? It was fun. Can't say I saw too much of the game, though.

2. My talent routine is a crowd pleaser.

Evidence: I tested it out today at the match. Well, I had to do something to keep us entertained while a bunch of guys dressed all in white stood around doing nothing except occasionally chasing after a tiny red ball, didn't I?

3. Beamer has talents of his own.

Evidence: ;);)

* * *

Today was a pretty good day. I had a lot of fun at the cricket (I *know*!) with Leila and her friends. Mum is still being super nice to me. Eva hasn't been around. The only dark spot in the picture is that Anna seems unhappy again. Maybe it was because we were at the cricket, which she hates more than I do. I don't know. I didn't really get a chance to ask her about it, either. We didn't have any time alone all day, and she went to bed before I did. When I whispered her name in the dark, she didn't respond. Which means she was either asleep or pretending to be. I'll try to talk to her tomorrow.

Beamer and I watched our final movie starring The Rock tonight. Well, most of it, at least (ahem). That's the great movie challenge done. We haven't revealed our scores yet, because we have to tally them. We're going to do the big reveal tomorrow night, at the carnival.

I've realized we probably should have got an impartial judge to score these movies, because there's no way Beamer's not going to cheat. And I'm determined not to let him win. But I gotta be honest, I've enjoyed the whole thing way more than I thought I would.

Of course, The Rock is still no Arnold Schwarzenegger.

Oh, I've added one more thing to my list:

1. My eyes.
2. My eyebrows.
3. My ears.
4. My hair.
5. My fingernails.
6. My boobs.
7. My forearms.
8. My smile.
9. That bit of neck just below my ear, next to my jaw.

That's it. Nothing to see here. Move along, DJ.

Sunday, 31 December

1 thing I discovered today:

1. Everything sucks. Including me. Most of all, me.

Evidence: I just can't right now, DJ. I can't.

Monday, 1 January

1 thing I discovered today:

1. Home is a mess, but at least it's just a literal mess, and not a metaphorical one like the one I left back in the Bay, which is much harder to clean up than some grimy dishes.

Evidence: I'm back home. With Dad. Are you surprised, DJ? He certainly was when I rocked up in the middle of the night. It looks like he hasn't cleaned since we left. Mum will NOT be impressed. Add that to the list.

* * *

Hey, DJ. Happy New Year! Here's hoping it's better than the last. Well, the last few weeks, anyway.

The thing is...I was actually having a good time for a little while there. Feeling positive about life. About myself. I was looking forward to that absurd pageant. Having fun with friends. Having fun with *Beamer*. My mum liked me for a change. Things weren't perfect, but they were good.

I was kidding myself.

I know what you're thinking. "What the hell happened?!" Right? Well, lucky for you, I want to tell you. I need to get it out of my head. Out of my heart. Just out of me.

You might remember that yesterday was the day my interview about the pageant was supposed to go live. It feels so long ago already (it *was* last year, har har!).

It was raining, so a group of us were back at Jo's, making our way through the *Mad Max* series. Everyone else had only seen the latest one, which was frankly offensive. It was a good distraction from the nerves that were twisting my gut as I refreshed the news page on my phone every five minutes, waiting for my interview to go up. Leila eventually grabbed my phone from me and told me to chill, but then she just started the refresh routine herself.

We were halfway through *Road Warrior* when she squealed and said, "It's up!"

You know, on top of everything else, it really pisses me off that *Road Warrior* is tainted for me forever now. It's my second favourite *Mad Max* after *Fury Road*, and I'll never be able to watch it in the same way again. Ugh.

But back to yesterday.

My heart was doing a mad dance in my chest as Leila Chrome-cast the interview to Jo's TV so we could all watch it on the big screen. And there was my grinning face in the thumbnail, larger than life. The title read: LOCAL PAGEANT LETS IN PLUS SIZE TEEN TO SHUT DOWN CRITICS.

My heart stopped dancing and started dropping toward my stomach region.

Leila pressed play.

On the screen, I began walking up the beach, looking out to the ocean thoughtfully, like I was a contestant on *The Bachelor*, while Sarah, the journalist who'd interviewed me, spoke in voiceover: "*Meet Maisie Martin, the sixteen-year-old girl breaking beauty standards to become the first ever plus-size contestant to participate in the Cobbers Bay Miss Teen Queen pageant.*"

I felt cold all over.

"I never thought I'd actually get through," the me on screen was saying, a desperate smile on her/my face.

Cut to Janice, the chirpy pageant lady, dressed in a shoulder-padded suit that was probably the hot new look in 1992, her teased and sprayed hair tied at the nape of her neck. She was saying something (chirpily) about bringing the pageant into the twenty-first century and how *"beauty comes in all sizes, so we're thrilled to have Maisie as our first plus-size contestant. Just thrilled."*

My head felt fuzzy and my stomach churned. The room around me got very quiet and very still.

On the screen, footage of my sister—thin, beautiful, smiling a dazzling (not desperate) smile—played, while through my haze I caught the words *"beauty queens run in the family"* and *"pressure to conform,"* before the screen switched back to my face, caught in a moment where I'd been unable to sustain that smile, looking down. I looked up a second later, a grin that was more like a grimace plastered on my face, squeaking out something about how honored I was just to be there.

I wanted to be sick. I wanted to faint. I wanted to get the fuck out of there.

So that's how I'd got in. It wasn't a fluke. It wasn't a mistake. It was so much worse.

I was the token fatty.

There was more to the video, but by that stage I

wasn't really taking anything in. I could feel everyone in the room glancing my way, sensing my silent freak-out in their midst.

When the video was over, I felt people gathering around me and heard voices talking all at once. Distantly, I registered words: "...you okay?...wasn't so bad...fuck 'em...give her some space...what's going on...isn't this good?...you'll show them...give her some space!"

Hands in mine, pulling me up. Arms around me, guiding me outside.

Gray sky above me. Gasping for breath.

Deep breaths. In, out. In, out.

Slowly coming back to myself.

When I resurfaced, I looked up to see Beamer's worried face looming above mine. Realized Leila's arm was around me, holding me up. Saw Anna kneeling in front of me, hand on my leg. Sebastian hovering behind her, concern marking his features.

Oh god. How embarrassing.

"Don't be silly, babe," Leila said. "Nothing to be embarrassed about." Oops. I'd said that out loud.

"Are you alright, Maise?" This was from Sebastian.

"I guess," I lied.

"What was that about?" Anna asked.

I looked around, searching for an answer that I

didn't really have yet. Everyone was looking at me intently, except for Beamer. He'd turned away and was leaning against the railing of Jo's veranda, looking out toward the ocean.

"I dunno," I said. "That was awful."

"I thought it was great, Maise! You spoke really well," Anna said.

I winced. As though he sensed my discomfort, Sebastian tapped Beamer on the shoulder and gestured with his head toward the steps leading away from Jo's house. Beamer silently followed him, shooting me a tight smile as he left.

That was the moment I burst into tears. Leila squeezed me tighter.

"What's wrong?" Anna said.

"They don't want me. Nobody wants me," I said with a sob.

"Of course they do! That's what that whole video was about! You're making history!"

I shook my head, my throat burning with the emotion I was trying to get under control. She didn't understand. I didn't want to make history. I just wanted to be like everyone else.

All my life, I've been different. I just wanted to fit in. In so many ways, I just wanted to *fit*. But I never could. And no one would ever let me forget it.

"Fuck 'em!" Leila was saying. "Who needs them and their ridiculous beauty standards? Fuck. Them."

"You've been hanging around me too long," Jo said from the doorway. She stepped in front of me, leaning against the railing. "You okay?"

I nodded, not really okay, but beginning to feel somewhat cried out.

Jo smiled. "Forget about the lot of them. Let's go have some fun."

* * *

We agreed to meet up at the carnival in an hour or so. We needed to get glam, which for me meant applying at least five hundred layers of makeup before I was ready to face the world. To be honest, all I really wanted to do was curl up in a ball in bed and never get up again, but the girls convinced me I'd feel better if I got out and distracted myself, and I knew they were right.

When Anna and I walked into the cabin, Mum was hunched over her phone. Laura was on the lounge next to her, saying something that she quickly cut off as soon as we walked in. Without a word, Mum got up and squeezed me tight, holding on to my arms as she pulled away and looked into my face with concern on her own.

"Missy-May, don't you worry about those comments. Don't you listen to any of them. A bunch of no-life loser trolls, that's what they are. You have every right to be in that pageant, and you know what? You're going to win it. You're beautiful, Maisie. Beautiful, do you hear me?" By this stage, she was squeezing my arms a little too tight.

"Comments?" I squeaked out.

"Seb and Beamer were just here—they mentioned you were upset," Laura said, a look of sympathy on her face.

"But what comments are you talking about?" I could feel the panic rising again as suspicion grew in me. Surely it couldn't get worse.

Ha. Of course it could.

I got out my phone and found the video on Facebook. Sure enough, there were already dozens of comments on it. There were some positive ones, but plenty that weren't.

Fat dog.

What's her talent, eating 20 burgers in one sitting?

Gross. No one wants to see that.

I couldn't read on. Literally, because tears were blurring my sight. Turns out I wasn't all cried out. Not by a long shot. For the first time in years, I collapsed into my mum's arms and sobbed my shattered heart out.

"It's not too late to cancel your entry," Mum said after a while. "This was exactly what I was worried about when you said you wanted to enter. I knew it would just upset you. If you'd only—"

I pulled away, shaking my head. I didn't want to hear the rest. I didn't want to think about it anymore.

"Anna and I are going to the carnival," I said.

Mum raised her eyebrows at the abrupt subject change. She opened her mouth to say something but hesitated. Finally, she said, "I think that's a great idea. Have some fun." She looked over at Laura. "We might see you there, hmmm? We were just about to head down with the twins."

"Yeah, maybe," I said. *I sure hope not*, I thought. I wanted a parent-free, worry-free, just all-round-free night.

Which goes to show you how truly foolish I am.

* * *

I was finishing my eyebrows when I noticed it. I'd stepped back from the mirror to check my handiwork, and its reflection caught my eye. A slip of paper, half tucked under my pillow.

It looked like it had been torn from a notebook. It was folded in half, and my name was scrawled on one side in messy boy handwriting. I opened it up. And... whoa.

I was glad Anna was in the shower at that moment. I don't know what I would have done if I'd opened it while she was there.

Then again, it might have saved me from doing the most terrible thing I've ever done. EVER.

But I'll get to that.

There, in more of that messy writing—writing that hadn't much improved since I'd secretly read it all those years ago—was a poem. A poem...for me?

A poem *about* me. About my body. About how *beautiful* my body was.

Sebastian Lee...had written me a poem.

For the first time since that morning, the knot in my stomach began to unravel and butterflies took up residence in its place. I was tearing up again, but this time, mixed in with the shame and self-hatred, there were feelings of gratitude and hope and, well, a lot of confusion.

At the bottom of the paper was the message: *Meet me in front of the main stage of the carnival at 5.*

It was four forty-five.

"Maise, you know, I'm not feeling too great, maybe I should stay in," Anna was saying as she walked in wearing a towel, her hair hanging damp around her shoulders.

Anna, who was my best friend.

Anna, who was with Sebastian.

Sebastian, the boy I'd been in love with for years.

Sebastian, the boy who'd just written me a poem and made me feel light when I was in a really dark place.

Unable to stop myself, I mumbled, "Um, I just remembered I have to give Leila something, I'll be back in fifteen." I rushed out the door.

The carnival was a ten-minute walk from the cabin. I made it there in six.

As I pushed my way through the crowd—mostly families with little kids at this hour—I saw him, standing in front of the main stage.

He was actually there.

Our eyes locked, and he smiled. I closed the distance between us, my heart threatening to thud its way right out of my chest.

"You got it then," Sebastian said, more of a statement than a question.

"Yeah," I said, holding up the note. I was panting because I'd run half the way and also because I wasn't sure I'd ever be able to breathe properly again.

"This should be interesting." He pulled out his phone and typed something. Then he looked up at me and said, "How are you, Maise?"

203

"Okay." Pant. "Better now."

He smiled. "Listen, you're gorgeous...you know that, right? Don't let a bunch of dickheads on the internet—or anyone else—let you believe otherwise. I swear, if those trolls were standing in front of me right now—well, they wouldn't be standing for long."

It was something about the way he said "dickhead" that did it. All those years of yearning, all those pent-up feelings, coursed through my body like a tidal wave. Starting low and spreading through every limb before finally bursting through my lips. Unleashed by a poem and a "dickhead."

I stepped forward, grabbed his face, and mashed it against mine in a kiss.

A kiss.

I was kissing Sebastian Lee.

I was kissing Sebastian Lee.

Sebastian Lee...was not kissing me.

His hands were on my shoulders, pushing me back. I opened my eyes and saw confusion and embarrassment and...pity?...in his.

"Maisie—"

Whatever he was about to say was cut off by the speaker we were standing near suddenly blaring to life. The opening chords of "(I've Had) The Time of My Life" from *Dirty Dancing* caught my attention, and I looked up. A figure all in black had appeared on stage.

Was that...Beamer?

It was Beamer.

And he was dancing.

Dancing.

He had a look of concentration on his face, and he was totally offbeat, but he was dancing. When he reached the front of the stage, he paused and bent forward, crooking his finger at me.

"Nobody puts Maisie in the corner," he called out.

Oh. Oh my god. Oh my shitting fucking god.

I felt cold all over. On stage, Beamer straightened, but he was still smiling. Vaguely I registered people around us stopping to see what was going on.

"Come on, Maisie Martin, you're not gonna leave me hanging here, are you?" Beamer said.

I couldn't move. I couldn't speak. I don't think I was even breathing.

The song played on.

And Beamer's smile slowly dropped, giving way to confusion. I watched as his gaze moved from me to Sebastian, still standing close to me, still resting one of his hands on my shoulder. Sebastian seemed to register this at the same time as me, because he pulled away. He stepped toward the stage and spoke quietly. I couldn't hear what he said, but it made Beamer's eyes flick back to me. And I saw something in them then that I'd never seen there before.

Hurt. He was hurt. And I was humiliated.

In that moment, I did the only thing I could think to do.

I turned and ran.

* * *

Oh boy, did I run. Literally, I ran back to the cabin. Metaphorically, I ran *wee wee wee* all the way home (in the passenger seat of my mum's car).

Oh yeah. You thought that was the worst of it, that whole humiliating litany of seriously bad, no-good, embarrassing events? Ha! Surely you know me better than that by now, DJ.

I stole Mum's car.

Well. Does it count as stealing if you have the keys? What about if you're not driving?

I think it probably does.

Mum definitely thinks it does. She's furious.

But I'm getting ahead of myself.

When I got back to the cabin, Mum and Laura were nowhere to be seen, but Anna was in the bedroom, dressed and shoving something into her backpack.

She looked up guiltily when I entered. I found out why later. In that moment, I barely even registered what she was doing. I was too caught up in my own emotions. My own mixed-up, overwhelming emotions. I didn't know what I was feeling.

Everything. Nothing.

One thing: I had to get out of there. I wanted to disappear. I needed to go home.

"What's wrong?" Anna asked, her brow furrowing. How could I tell Anna what had just happened? She'd hate me, like Sebastian probably did. Like Beamer definitely did.

"I want to go home," I said. "I've had enough."

She contemplated me for a moment. I was crying, like really ugly-crying, all snotty and slobbery and gross.

"So let's go," Anna said.

I nearly choked. "What?"

"Let's get out of here. Everyone's out for the night. They probably won't even notice that we're gone until tomorrow. By that time, you'll be safely at home with your dad. What are they going to do?"

The plan was appealing. "But how?"

"We can borrow your mum's car. I've got my permit, I can drive."

"But how will she—"

"Come on, Maise. Let's do it. Or would you rather be stuck here for another week?"

I should have been suspicious. I should have questioned her motives. But right then I was too focused on trying to hide mine. I needed to escape. It was too tempting to resist.

And that's how I ended up spending New Year's Eve in a stolen car, with my best friend in the driver's seat, and all my worries receding behind me.

Except that's not really true, is it? About leaving my worries behind. Because the thing about worries is, they're in your head, and they tend to follow you around wherever you go, like a vicious little puppy that won't stop biting at your ankles (only far less cute).

Still, at least I wouldn't have to face everyone and relive the mortification of the past few days over and over again. At least I could pretend.

Oh, who am I kidding? I only made things worse.

DJ, I really fucked up.

Tuesday, 2 January

2 things I discovered today:

1. The Rock has starred in way too many freaking action movies.

Evidence: I tried to find a decent one on Netflix that DIDN'T star him, and it was basically impossible. I ended up skipping the genre altogether and going on a horror binge. I probably won't sleep tonight...not that I would have anyway.

2. I've updated my list of things I like about myself.

Evidence: See below.

* * *

Hey, DJ, here's a list of things I like about myself:

Wednesday, 3 January

1 thing I discovered today:

1. I don't know if things will ever be the same between me and Anna again. I don't know that I want them to be, either.

Evidence: Anna came around today and we had a big, long talk. It helped. But everything is still weird.

* * *

If you're feeling like you're missing something right about now, DJ, it might be because you are. It was all getting to be too much the other day, so I kind of skipped over the bit about me and Anna. You know, the post-stealing my mum's car bit.

The bit where we were stuck in a car for eight hours together.

The bit where *everything* came out.

We were about four hours into our little adventure when I started to have major second thoughts. The visions of the video, and the trolls, and the look on Sebastian's face...and the look on Beamer's face...and everything else were slowly being replaced with the inevitable sight of my mum absolutely blowing her top when she discovered us—and her car—gone.

Until that point, it had been kind of fun. Exhilarating. We blasted angry music and screamed and laughed. We stopped for snacks and terrible gas station coffee. We didn't talk much, but it felt like for once I might actually be in a movie. It was freeing.

Still, something had been gnawing at me. I think it was guilt. And fear. Not to mention a healthy dose of regret—not just for what I'd done that day, but for what I was currently doing. And it built and built and built until—

"We have to turn back," I said.

Anna glanced at me but didn't respond.

"Anna! Come on. We've had our fun. Now we have to go back."

"Are you serious? We're nearly home!"

"We're still hours away. Let's go back. It's not too late. Like you said, no one will have even noticed we're missing." I'd messaged Leila and said I couldn't go to the carnival because I was feeling too shit, and she'd replied saying she hoped I was okay and she'd see me tomorrow (that was one of the things that had been gnawing at me). I knew Anna had messaged Sebastian to say we were staying in. I hadn't told her yet that he probably would have understood our absence even if she hadn't said a thing.

"Anna?"

She kept her eyes on the road.

"*Anna?*"

"We're not going back, Maisie. Now is not the time to grow some balls."

"What's that supposed to mean?"

"This is your MO, right? You run away and hide. From everything."

"What are you talking about?"

"Remember that time in Year 8 when Pete O'Grady wanted to ask you out, and you went and hid in the toilets? I had to come and physically drag you out. Because a boy *liked* you!"

"He didn't like me. He liked you," I mumbled.

"He was asking you out!"

"To get closer to you!"

She shot her eyes my way. There was real anger in them now. It singed me.

"What about when we were supposed to do that

group presentation in Year 10 English, but you totally bailed at the last minute?"

"I was sick." I *had* been sick. With fear about standing in front of everyone. I thought she understood that.

"Or how about two weeks ago, when you went MIA for a whole day, even though *you* brought me along on this goddamn trip, and I had to hang out with *your* family and friends all by myself? And now, the one time I'm actually on board with you running and hiding, you want to chicken out."

I narrowed my eyes. "Why are you so desperate to get home, anyway?"

She kept her mouth shut at that, staring straight ahead again.

"Anna?"

She sighed. "Look. Dan's been messaging me. He feels really bad about everything and he wants to get back together. He's at this New Year's party tonight, and I was kinda hoping to get to him by midnight... you know, be all romantic." A shadow of a smile passed over her face.

Something had been building in my chest as she spoke. Something tight and hard. Something a lot like rage.

"Dan?" I said, very quietly.

She glanced at me. "Yeah."

"Dan. The Dickhead?"

She rolled her eyes. "Grow up, Maisie."

The rage exploded.

"Are you serious, Anna? Are you fucking serious?"

"What?!"

"What about all the shit he pulled on you?"

"He's changed."

"He cheated on you!"

"He regrets it."

I took a deep breath, trying to get a handle on my fury.

"What about Sebastian?" I said with only a slight quiver in my voice.

She shrugged. "It was just a hookup. Nothing serious."

I was shaking. *Just a hookup?!*

The words spilled out of me before I could stop them. "Oh. I guess you won't mind that I kissed him, then."

Now she was shocked. "You *what*? When? How?"

"Just before we left," I said. "When I went out. I was meeting him."

Her mouth dropped open and she laughed, but there was no humor in it.

"Oh my god, you are such a hypocrite! Trying to

make me feel bad and acting like Dan is the worst person in the world, when here you are making out with your best friend's boyfriend?"

"I thought it was just a hookup," I said, a tone of mock sweetness in my voice.

She was shaking her head. "I knew it. I *knew* you still had a thing for him! Insisting it was okay when really you were just waiting for your chance."

"If you knew I still had a thing for him, why did you steal him from me?"

"You kind of have to have something in the first place for it to be stolen," she spat out.

My head snapped back reflexively, my body reacting as though I'd been physically slapped.

I didn't have much to say to that.

We spent the rest of the trip in bitter silence.

* * *

When we finally reached home it was after 1 AM. Dan the Dickhead was already there, sitting on the curb in front of my house, waiting for Anna. I guess she'd texted him from the road at some point. She ran straight into his arms and they took off, leaving me standing on my porch alone. The house was dark and quiet. I tried to figure out what would scare Dad less—using my keys to let myself into the house or knocking on the door so he'd have to get up.

I went with the door knock. My stomach churned. He'd probably think something terrible had happened. Like, more terrible than what *had* happened which, while definitely terrible, suddenly seemed a bit trivial standing there alone in the dark, in the early hours of the new year.

I'll never forget the look of panic on Dad's face when he opened the door, still bleary-eyed from sleep. He looked like he hadn't shaved in weeks.

"What's happened?! Your mum? Eva?"

"Everyone's fine," I said. I couldn't hold back a sob. "I'm sorry, Dad. I'm really sorry. I just wanted to be home."

He drew me into his arms and for the second time in that long, awful day, I cried in a parent's arms like I was five years old again.

I didn't give Dad the whole story, just enough so that he understood why I might have shown up on the doorstep in the middle of the night (though I don't think he fully got it; then again, neither do I). He called Mum—just as Anna had predicted, she was still out with Laura and hadn't even realized I was gone. I swear I could hear her scream all the way from Cobbers Bay—and not just through the phone line.

They argued that night. And then the next day. They couldn't decide what to do with me. What to do with the car. How to get Mum home.

Like I said: I really fucked up.

* * *

Which brings me to today. Dad's back at work. Mum's intermittently sending me messages about how much trouble I'm in. Leila's sending me constant messages asking if I'm okay and tagging me in cute animal pictures and ridiculous memes to make me laugh. Eva has tried calling me a few times and even sent me a message telling me to come back. Anna, meanwhile, has been radio silent.

This morning, I decided to bite the bullet. I messaged Anna and asked her to come over. *We need to talk*, I said, like some bad breakup line from a movie.

In a way, it kind of was a breakup. Not from Anna, not completely. But from our old friendship. Things haven't been great lately. But I've been thinking: when were they ever *truly* great?

I mean, sure, we've had moments of greatness. Times when my sides ached and my face hurt from laughing so much. Where I've felt exhilarated and alive and more connected to Anna than anyone else in my life.

But in between those moments? I've always felt one step behind. Like any second I could do the wrong thing and be left alone.

I'm not saying it's Anna's fault. I think a lot of it comes down to my own insecurities. The way I never feel good enough.

But I've realized something in the past couple of weeks. I never felt that way with Leila. Or...or Beamer. And it was such a relief. A release from a pain I didn't even realize I'd been feeling.

I think the blowup between me and Anna the other night was probably a long time coming. As was the conversation we had today.

"I'm really sorry, Maise," she said when she got here. I believed her. It just wasn't enough.

"Sorry for what?" I said.

"For...the other night. For getting you in trouble. I'm in trouble too." My mum had called Anna's mum and they'd got into a huge argument, which just made Mum even more furious with me.

"Anything else?" I asked.

Anna twisted her lips and looked around the room like she was searching for the right answer. She sighed. "Yeah...I'm sorry for everything. For...for Seb, I guess."

I nodded, trying not to cry. I'd done enough of that in the last few days.

"I knew…I knew you liked him," Anna continued. "But I was feeling really shit after everything with Dan, and he was being so nice and I felt like I deserved some happiness, you know? And…and I didn't think you really had a chance with him, so I thought I may as well take mine."

Aaaaand there went the tears.

Anna scooted closer to me on the bed and put her arm around me. "I'm so sorry, Maise."

I shook my head, swallowing down my sobs. "I'm sorry too. I shouldn't have kissed Seb on New Year's. For so many reasons. Including the fact you were with him. But Anna…I was hurt. You really hurt me."

"But you said it was fine."

I shrugged her off. "You didn't believe that, not for one second."

"Why did you say it was okay, then?" She was getting angry now.

"Because you're my friend! Because I wanted you to be happy! Because…I didn't think I really had a chance with him, either."

"So how can you be mad at me when you thought the exact same thing?"

I exhaled a huff of air out of my nose in a frustrated, not-really-a-laugh laugh. "Because you're my friend! You're supposed to want me to be happy too."

She raised her eyebrows. "But what's going to make you happy, Maisie?"

"I don't know," I whispered, rubbing my face.

"Well let me know when you do, okay?" She got up to leave.

Before she got through the door I called for her to wait.

"I don't want to fight anymore," I said.

"Me either."

We were quiet for a moment, then she said, "So what do we do?"

I looked up at her. I'd been so envious and angry at her without even knowing it. Or I'd known it, but I'd refused to acknowledge it. I'd pretended the feelings weren't there. I couldn't go on pretending.

"I think it's going to take time," I said. "We've just got to give it some time."

"Time," she said, chewing on the word before swallowing it. She bent down to give me a hug. "Okay. Time it is."

Thursday, 4 January

2 things I discovered today:

1. My dad is a gutless wonder.

Evidence: I sprung him in a huge lie that he's been hiding from all of us for months.

2. I'm a gutless wonder too.

Evidence: My whole life, my mum's told me I'm just like my dad. I've always been quite proud of that. But today...not so much.

* * *

DJ, you are never going to believe what I discovered today. My dad, the gutless wonder.

I thought I'd surprise him for lunch. Oh boy, did I surprise him. Surprised the security guard at the front desk of his office too.

"Maisie? What are you doing here?" Donna said. Without waiting for me to answer, she continued, "Do you need to pick up something for your dad? I'm afraid he'll have to come in himself when everyone is back from the holidays. I can't let you in. Sorry, it's protocol."

"Back...from the holidays?"

A puzzled look crossed Donna's face. "Yeah, the office is closed. Like it is every year. You know that."

"But what about..." My brain was trying to put together the pieces, but I felt like I was missing a big one.

"Haven't you seen your dad today?" Donna said.

"Yeah, this morning—before he left for work."

Donna looked confused. That made two of us. What was going on?

"Why don't you call your dad and see where he's at," she said finally, her face softening.

So that's what I did.

"Eminem! What's up? Hope you're not watching anything too terrible without me." Dad sounded really cheery.

"Hey, Dad, um, I wanted to surprise you at your office for lunch and—"

"Oh, sorry, Em, I'm flat out today, I can't."

"But I'm at your office now. Where are you? Donna says—"

"You're at the office?" His voice suddenly lost its cheer.

"Yeah, like I said, but Donna says you're not here. That no one is. What's going on?"

After a moment of silence, he sighed and said, "Meet me at home, okay? I'll...I'll explain everything. See you there in twenty minutes." And he hung up.

I looked at the phone and then up at Donna, my face clearly showing the horror I felt, judging by the sympathy on her own.

I hurried home, feeling sick, my mind racing. What the hell was going on?

It must be an affair, I thought. What else could it be?

The good news is it wasn't an affair.

The bad news is—well, you'll see.

Dad was already home when I got there. He was sitting on the lounge, his head in his hands. He looked utterly defeated.

"Dad?" I hurried to sit next to him. "Dad, what's going on?"

He didn't say anything.

"Dad, you're scaring me."

He let out a heavy sigh. "Oh, Maisie. What am I going to do?"

"What's happened? Tell me."

And he finally did. He explained how, after months of rumors swirling that there were going to be huge cutbacks at work, he'd been called in to a meeting with his boss.

"I thought they either had to be giving me a raise, or firing me," he said with a grimace.

They were firing him. Well, making him redundant. Apparently there's a difference. Redundancy isn't as bad as firing, in the sense that you didn't do anything wrong, but your job isn't needed anymore. *You're* not needed anymore.

It sounded kinda worse to me.

I think it sounded worse to Dad too. He said he couldn't face telling Mum. Telling any of us. He was humiliated. Depressed. It had happened in November. I was stressed about school, Mum was in the middle of her annual pre-Christmas shopping frenzy. We were all looking forward to the holidays. He didn't want to ruin that. He'd tell us after, he decided. When he'd found another job. His redundancy payout meant we were okay for money, for now. It was his pride that hurt the most. And his hope for the future.

"No one's hiring," he said. His face was in his hands

again. "At least, not someone like me. What am I going to do? I'm too old to start over."

I didn't know how to answer that. And I had questions of my own.

"But what were you doing all those days you said you were at work?" Even though he'd finished up in early December, he'd still been getting up, getting dressed as usual, out the door by 8 AM, home after 6 PM every night. Talking about all the stress at the office. Talking about the big project he was working on. I couldn't believe the lengths he'd gone to in order to hide the truth.

He huffed, sounding more bitter than I'd ever heard him in my life. "Went to the library. Went to the park. Went to the bar." Guilt was etched in every line on his face.

"Why couldn't you just tell us?!"

"I couldn't, Maisie. I couldn't."

"But why would you lie?" I was trying to stay calm—I could see how cut up he was—but I was pretty cut up myself.

"I'm sorry, I'm so sorry," was all he said.

"All that bullshit about having to work through the holidays, and you weren't even working at all! Why would you do that? Why?!"

"I just needed some space to myself, alright? To get

my head straight. A bit of Netflix therapy, you know?"
He was smiling a smile of camaraderie now. Tentative, but there.

I did know. It just made me angrier. Because he'd lied and he'd hid and he'd been a coward and he'd wanted to avoid hurting us, but really he just hurt us more. And that made me mad as hell.

But what made me absolutely ropeable was this: *I did know.* I got it.

"*You're just like your father,*" Mum's said to me countless times, usually accompanied with a sigh and a shake of her head. And it's the truth. What I had done, the way I had run, wasn't so different to what Dad was doing. Trying to avoid problems. Fleeing rather than facing people head on.

I've lied. I've hidden. I've been a coward. And the person I've hurt the most is probably myself.

"We've both got to stop running," I said finally.

Friday, 5 January

3 things I discovered today:

1. It really is better to face things rather than run away. I know I said I discovered this a couple of weeks ago, but I guess the lesson didn't quite sink in. Not enough. Maybe it will now.

Evidence: Not to jinx things but...everything is starting to look up.

2. Sour apple slurpees are not a good idea.

Evidence: My taste buds, via a random gas station that didn't have raspberry flavor (wtf).

3. I actually don't mind some of Dad's music.

Evidence: I listened to a lot of it today. I especially like Crowded House. Just don't tell Dad.

* * *

Guess where I am, DJ!

Go on, guess.

I'll give you a few more seconds to think about it.

Three.

Two.

One.

Ding ding ding! If you guessed I'm right back at Cobbers Bay, you've won the grand prize of being right! It's a good feeling, isn't it?

Yes, we drove back to Cobbers Bay. Dad and I. Not Anna and I. Anna stayed home, with Dan the I'm-no-longer-supposed-to-call-him-a-dickhead-because-they're-fully-back-together-but-I-still-think-he's-a-dickhead-Dickhead. I haven't seen her since our big talk the other day. Time, and all that.

Meanwhile I'll have to plant a tree to make up for all the extra gas my shenanigans have wasted this week.

Shenanigans. Isn't that a great word? That's how Mum described my week. Right after she grounded me until I'm thirty.

But I'm getting ahead of myself. Let me take you back.

You remember how Dad fessed up, right? Of course

228

you do, it only happened yesterday. Anyway, we talked about how he had to tell Mum the truth, and he couldn't do it over the phone. Since she was kind of stranded in Cobbers Bay thanks to me, Dad figured we could kill all our birds (metaphorical birds, I'd never kill actual birds—not even those myna birds that Grandpa says are rats with wings) with one stone (metaphorical stone, literal car) and just drive to Cobbers Bay together. Of course, this meant I'd have to face some demons of my own. I needed to, I knew that now. I was still shitting bricks. Dad was too.

We agreed that dragging it out would only make things worse, so we joined hands and bravely rode into the belly of the beast together.

The drive itself was actually kind of nice. We spent the whole time talking, as if to make up for the distance and the silence of the last couple of weeks. I think we were also avoiding getting lost in our own thoughts. I know I was.

I told him properly about everything that's been going on. (Well, not *everything*. Some of it is strictly NSFP—not safe for parents.) It hit me all over again how much I'd missed having him around.

Here's Dad's take on it all (the condensed version):

Eva: "I just want her to be happy. I want you both to be happy."

Mum: "We're *not* getting a divorce. At least, not if I can help it. Your mum is the most important thing in the world to me, next to you kids. But I've really messed up this time. I hope she can forgive me."

Anna: "People change. Friendships change. You guys will figure it out. Or not. But you'll be okay."

Beamer: "Terrible taste in movies, never speak to him again." (I only told Dad the bit about the movie challenge. The rest is totally NSFP!)

Seb: Um, most definitely NSFP! WAY TOO EMBARRASSING!!

Leila: "She sounds delightful, can't wait to meet her. If I survive your mother, that is."

The beauty pageant: "You're not gonna let some wankers on the internet stop you from doing something you want to do, are you? Don't give them that power, Em. That power is all yours."

My dad. He's alright sometimes.

* * *

We arrived in the Bay just before dinner.

Mum came rushing out of the cabin when we pulled up. I was barely out of the car when she grabbed me and said, "Maisie Martin! You're never leaving my sight again! Not until you're at least thirty! You are

230

so grounded. I never expected such shenanigans from you." But she gave me the tightest hug she's ever given me in my life.

Dad appeared at the front of the car. Mum pulled away, and their eyes met. I held my breath and didn't let it out until Mum walked over to Dad, placed her hands on his face, and said, "I've missed you, you bastard."

Dad held her for a moment. Then he pulled away and said, "We've got a lot to talk about."

He asked her to go for a walk with him down to the rock pools. I knew it was their favorite place, but I wondered if it was a wise idea for him to break the news to her in such an isolated, rocky, watery spot. Seemed like he was making it easy for her to murder him if she didn't take it well.

But I kept my mouth shut.

* * *

Another guessing game: this one's called guess who showed up while Mum and Dad were gone?

No, it wasn't Beamer. Why would you think it was him?

It wasn't Seb, either.

It was Eva. My darling older sister.

She wanted to talk. Suddenly everyone in my family wants to talk.

Maybe I should talk too. I'll tell you something that I've never told anyone, DJ. Something you should understand before I go on.

I've mentioned before how Eva and I both used to dance, right? We were even going to enter the pageant together. It was a whole thing.

Until Eva decided it shouldn't be anymore. That I wasn't good enough.

It happened when I was thirteen. I was still dancing then. But I wasn't loving it. It was always something I'd been able to lose myself in. I could switch my brain off and just enjoy my body for a change. Leave behind the discomfort that haunted every other moment of my life.

As I got older, it became harder and harder to lose myself.

That year, I'd put on a lot of weight. I'd always been chubby, but now I'd really stacked it on.

My dance teacher told me I had to lose weight. Mum put me on a diet. I wore two sports bras to try to strap down my boobs, like that'd make a difference.

I felt the whispers of the other girls behind my back. That was bad enough. But the ones who said shit to my face were worse.

"You're a disgusting, fat pig. You don't belong in public, let alone on stage," Matilda Johnson, the meanest of them all, said to me one day. The girls around her laughed and oinked at me.

I almost quit then. But I didn't—because of Eva.

Because when I told her what had happened, she said those girls were just jealous. She said I was a great dancer. She said she *loved* dancing with me.

Because when we danced together, we were perfectly in sync. Connected. Sisters.

It didn't matter that our bodies didn't match. Our movements did.

Or so I'd thought.

That year, when we came to Cobbers Bay, I mentioned entering the pageant to Eva. We were both finally old enough to be in it together. Like we'd talked about. She'd been waiting for it. I'd been looking forward to it. This was our year.

But she just shrugged. Gave me vague answers. Put me off.

I kept at her about it. "The deadline's soon, we're going to miss out," I said one day when we were at the beach, just the two of us. She was lying there reading and I was sitting next to her, eating hot chips covered in chicken salt. I held the bag under her nose, offering her some, but she didn't want any chips. She didn't want me, either. Only I didn't realize it at first, despite the fact that she kept reading her book, pretending not to hear me while I begged her to enter the pageant.

"Come on," I said. "Let's go do it now."

She ignored me.

"Eva."

Nothing.

"Eva!"

Still nothing.

"EVA!" I threw a chip at her.

"Cut it out, Maisie!"

"Finally, she speaks," I said. "So, do you want to enter or what?"

She rolled over, lying on her tummy and leaning on her elbows so she could still look at her book.

"I've already entered," she said quietly.

"What?"

"I've already entered," she said, louder this time.

"For both of us?"

"Just for me." Quiet again.

"Oh. So...should I go enter?"

She paused, then said, "Do you really think that's a good idea?"

"What do you mean?"

"I mean...I don't think you'd get through."

"Why not?"

Even though she had dark sunnies on, I could tell she was giving me a look. I dropped my head, staring at the hot chips, my appetite vanishing.

"Are you ashamed of me?"

Nothing.

"Are you?!"

"No. I just...I want to win, okay? I need to win."

"But what about..." I trailed off as she stared down at her book again. "You're such a bitch!" Tears were stinging my eyes.

She snorted. "It's not my fault you can't control yourself."

"You *are* ashamed of me!"

"Do you blame me, Maisie? You're ashamed of yourself! All you ever do is complain. But you do nothing about it. You don't want people to call you a disgusting, fat pig? Then stop acting like one. You expect me to dance with you, but you could barely keep up with me before, and look at you now! You *don't* belong on stage!"

What could I say to that? Nothing.

I stood up very slowly and walked away without a word.

I only just made it out of Eva's line of sight before I fell down sobbing.

She'd been my rock. But that day, she shattered me.

I didn't talk to her for the rest of our time off. She didn't talk to me either.

I told myself that it suited me fine, but the truth is it only hurt me more. As upset as I was, all it would have taken was one word from Eva—one "sorry"—and we might have been okay. I might have been okay.

All I wanted was something, anything, that showed she gave a damn about me. But I got nothing.

When we returned home, I told Mum I was quitting dancing once and for all.

Meanwhile Eva threw herself into it more than ever. It was hard to tell we weren't actually talking to each other, because it was so rare for us to even be in the same room. Dancing consumed Eva's life. It consumed our whole family.

When Eva moved to Melbourne, I felt relieved. Like maybe, finally, I'd be free from her and the gigantic shadow her skinny little body cast over me.

Our mutual silent treatment persisted.

Then Eva came out last year, and all of a sudden she wanted to be sisters again.

"I need you, Maise," she'd said.

But I'd needed her too. So badly. And I still hadn't forgiven her.

I said, "I don't care that you're gay. I feel the exact

same way about you today that I did yesterday. You're not my sister, and I don't ever want to talk to you again."

It was back to the silent treatment after that. Until, out of the blue, Eva started emailing me and sending me messages. Random stuff, about what she was doing that day, or something she'd seen that made her think of me. I ignored them all.

Which brings us pretty much up to date.

Now you know it all, DJ.

Except what happened today.

* * *

"Hey, I was hoping you'd be here," Eva said with a smile.

"Where's Bess?"

"She's at the Airbnb. I needed to do something on my own. It's...I wanted to talk to you, actually."

I nodded. I knew what was coming. I was ready.

"I'm sorry," we both said at once.

Eva's eyes widened. Tears sprung up in mine. And I did something I hadn't done in years. I got up and gave my sister a hug.

She was crying now as well. "I'm sorry," she said. "I'm so, so sorry."

"Me too," I said. And we laughed through our tears.

After a while, when we'd both settled down and Eva had made us cups of tea, we sat next to each other on the lounge and talked and talked.

"I was awful to you, Maise," she said. "I didn't really think about it at the time. I mean, I knew you were upset, but I was so caught up in my own shit. I was not in a good place. And I took it out on you. I'm sorry."

I'd been waiting to hear her say "sorry" for years, and now it seemed like she couldn't stop saying it.

"Do you remember Rachel?" Eva asked.

"Your friend from school?" Rachel had been one of Eva's best friends. She used to come over our place a lot, but then Eva got busy with dancing and Rachel stopped coming around. I didn't think much about it at the time.

Eva nodded. "You don't know this but...she was actually the first person I came out to."

"Oh?"

"Yeah. When I was sixteen."

"*Oh.*"

Eva sipped her tea and sighed. "I...I really liked her. Actually, I kind of loved her. And, well, let's just say she did not respond how I hoped she would. Quite the opposite."

Another "oh," was all I could manage.

"Between that," Eva went on, "and how much I was struggling at school—and just, I don't know, the general awfulness of being sixteen—" she shot me a knowing look "—I was a bit of a mess. And a total cow to you. I'm not trying to excuse it. There *is* no excuse. But I guess I just wanted to explain."

I nodded. I was finally beginning to understand.

"The thing with the pageant," she continued. "I felt like I needed a win, you know? But it backfired. Because I ended up losing in the worst way...I lost my baby sister." She reached for my hand, and I gave hers a squeeze. "I mean, you wouldn't talk to me even after I came out. I thought that was pretty fucked up."

"I'm sorry," I said. She waved her hand as if brushing my words away. She wasn't done yet.

"It took me a long time to realize how much I'd hurt you," she said. "It wasn't until I met Bess, really, that I fully got it. The essay I told you about, the one she wrote, that made me want to meet her? It was about all the terrible ways people had treated her because she's fat, but how she loved herself anyway. Her writing was so powerful...and I recognized myself in it. Not in the way she felt, but in the way she'd been treated. In how I'd seen people treat you. In how *I'd* treated you. Even when I was trying to be nice, I know I said things that hurt. I didn't get it then, but I do now. And I'm sorry, Maisie. Sorry that I made you feel like you weren't good enough."

I was tempted to crack a joke about how not everything revolved around her, but I stayed quiet. To tell you the truth, I was too full of emotion to speak a word.

Eva shoved my shoulder playfully. "I've been wanting to say all this for ages, but I never got a chance. You kept ignoring me."

At last, I was ready to talk.

I told her how upset I'd been. How much I appreciated everything she said today.

And I told her I was sorry.

All that time I'd been waiting for her to apologize—I hadn't realized how much I'd needed to say it too.

Because as much as Eva had hurt me, I'd also hurt her. She said she'd been caught up in her own shit, but I was the one so focused on my own problems, I'd never even stopped to consider what might be happening in her life. That it wasn't so perfect after all. That she was experiencing her own pain—and that I'd inflicted some of it myself.

Today, I saw Eva properly for the first time.

"You're my sister," I told her. "And I love you."

"You should talk to Beamer," Eva said later.

"What? Why?"

"I heard what happened. Poor guy."

"What? How?"

"He came to me last week. Said he wanted to learn that *Dirty Dancing* routine. Had this big grand plan to sweep you off your feet. Which didn't exactly pan out, it seems."

"*What?!*"

She laughed.

"Tell me everything," I said.

It turns out Eva and Beamer had been meeting in secret every day. He'd asked her to teach him to dance. Not so he could dance with her. So he could dance...with me.

My big freak-out on New Year's Eve had made him decide to move his grand gesture ahead of schedule. To cheer me up and make me smile. To remind me that there were people in the world—the only ones who mattered—who thought I was amazing and beautiful and worthy of dancing and beauty pageants and doing whatever the hell I wanted.

"Beamer said all this?"

Eva nodded. "Who knew he had it in him, hey? He's grown into a pretty great guy."

"And Seb?"

"Oh, he knew about the whole thing. Went along for moral support. Which I think is where your wires got crossed, hmmm?"

"Wait, so you know...?"

"I spoke to Beamer the other day. He was pretty cut up. Said you still loved Seb and he'd just been a distraction."

I stared down at my tea. I'd been doggedly avoiding thinking about everything that had happened with Beamer, but now it all came crashing in. I still couldn't believe that he—annoying, pain-in-the-butt Beamer—had planned what was probably the sweetest gesture I'd ever heard of in my life.

He'd tried to learn to dance for me.

He'd written a poem for me.

He'd...*oh my god, he'd written poetry.*

It had been Beamer all along.

I thought back to the look on his face when I told him I'd read Sebastian's poetry—which was actually *Beamer's* poetry all along.

"So...you really liked his poetry, hey?"

"There's someone that I like, which I think is pretty obvious."

"I dare you to kiss me."

"You're so beautiful."

It had been Beamer the entire time.

"So do you?" Eva interrupted my thoughts.

"Do I what?"

"Still love Seb?"

In that moment, I didn't know what I felt. Other than totally overwhelmed. All I could do was shrug.

"Well then, next question," Eva said. "And a more pressing one, I think: what are you going to do tomorrow?"

That one I had an answer for. I smiled.

"Tomorrow, I'm going to kick some Teen Queen butts," I said. "And I'm going to need your help."

* * *

I've really got to get some sleep, DJ. Beauty sleep for the beauty pageant, you know.

(Question: what's the difference between beauty sleep and ugly sleep? I feel like most people probably experience the latter.)

(I know, I know, it's about getting sleep so you *are* beautiful. Because if you don't sleep, you're haggard and ugly. Right?)

(I really need to get some sleep.)

(But I wanted to give you one final update.)

Mum and Dad.

They were gone for ages. And ages and ages. Eva and I had just ordered Thai for dinner when they finally rocked up.

They'd both been crying, I could tell.

They sat us down, looking very serious.

My heart was in my throat.

"Your father—" Mum started.

"I already told Eva everything," I interrupted.

"Good. That's good," Mum said. "Your father—"

"Please don't get a divorce." There was desperation in my voice. "He's sorry. He didn't mean it. He'll never do it again. He needs us. We need him."

Eva reached out and grabbed my hand.

Mum looked at us with wide, emotional eyes. "Your father and I...are *not* getting a divorce."

I breathed out a sigh of relief and squeezed Eva's hand. "So everything's alright?"

"Well, no, I wouldn't go that far," Mum said.

My heart constricted again.

"It's going to take time," Dad broke in. He looked at Mum.

She couldn't meet his eyes. "Yes. A lot of time," she said.

"But you understand, don't you, Mum?" Eva asked. I

got the feeling she was talking about more than Dad.

Mum paused for a minute, then got up to sit between Eva and me. She put her arms around us. "I might not yet...but I'll try to," she said. And she squeezed us both tight.

I looked over at Dad. He had tears in his eyes. I got up and hugged him.

Behind me, I heard Mum say, "Why don't you get Bess over for dinner?"

So Eva did.

And you know, it wasn't perfect. Mum wasn't talking to Dad. She had just started talking to me and Eva again (talking, not yelling). But we were all in the same room. A frosty room, yes, but with the smallest hint of thaw. It was a start. Which is much better than an ending.

Okay, now I really gotta get some sleep.

Saturday, 6 January

1 thing I discovered today:

1. What's that saying? You are braver than you believe, and stronger than you seem, and smarter than you think.

Evidence: I think it's from Winnie-the-Pooh. Is it Christopher Robin who says it? Whoever it was, they were speaking the truth.

* * *

What a day! Tell you all about it tomorrow, DJ.
   I'm too tired right now.
   DELIRIOUS.
   I'll just give you this quick update. Here's a list of things I like about myself:

1. My eyes.
2. My eyebrows.
3. My ears.
4. My hair.
5. My fingernails.
6. My boobs.
7. My forearms.
8. My smile.
9. That bit of neck just below my ear, next to my jaw.
10. My midriff.
11. My guts.
12. My dancing feet.
13. My heart.

Sunday, 7 January

1 thing I discovered today:

1. Life really isn't like the movies.

Evidence: This vacation. And, you know, LIFE.

* * *

Sorry if my handwriting is a bit all over the place, DJ. I'm in the car, on the way home. Yes, again! This time I'm in the back seat, and Mum's driving. Dad's in the passenger seat next to her. They're listening to Crowded House and talking every now and then. Not much, and not very warmly. But hey, it's progress.

We said goodbye to Eva and Bess this morning. Mum promised we'd go down to Melbourne in a month or two to visit them. I think she's trying to show Eva she's fine with the whole quitting dancing thing, even though I'm not sure she is. Not yet. But hey, it's progress.

We said goodbye to Leila and the others; to the Lees and Beamer this morning too.

But wait, I'm doing this all wrong. I'm telling you about today when there is still SO MUCH to tell you about yesterday. I really left you hanging there, didn't I, DJ? Sorry about that. It's just—so much has happened. Where do I begin?

Yesterday! PAGEANT DAY.

We got up at the crack of dawn (that's the second time in as many weeks for me, I'm practically a morning person!) to do my hair and makeup. Bess and Eva came around to help. We put some music on to set the mood, which Dad wasn't very happy about, since he was still trying to sleep. He got up and walked out in a bit of a huff, and Mum got that pinched dog's bum look on her face. But when he returned ten minutes later with coffees for us all, she softened, just a tiny bit.

We'd been at work for a little while when our tentative peace was threatening to explode.

"Not too poufy!" I was saying to Eva as she teased my hair. "No, no pink eyeshadow." I swatted Mum's hand away.

"That's it, everyone out," Bess said.

Mum and Eva both looked at her in surprise.

"Maisie and I have got this." She shooed them out the door, Mum muttering under her breath but, surprisingly, obeying.

"Alright." Bess turned to me with a smile. "Now tell me exactly what you want."

With skilled hands, she helped me get my hair into soft waves that I was happy with, and finished off my makeup with a perfect winged eyeliner and just the right amount of highlighter.

As she worked, we chatted. She told me about growing up in Melbourne and how she'd lived in Paris for a year when she turned eighteen. She asked me what I wanted to do after school and listened as I talked about how stressed I was about not having any idea. She said it was okay not to have it all figured out yet.

"Can I ask you something?" I said to her after a while.

She smiled as she leaned over me, ready to glue false lashes onto my eyelids. "You can ask me anything."

"How did you get to be so brave?" I closed my eyes.

"Brave?"

I swallowed hard. "Yeah, I mean...I'm kind of shitting myself right now. I've spent the past few years hiding and trying not to draw attention to myself...or my body. I've never even been brave enough to wear a bikini to the beach. And in a matter of hours I'm supposed to get up there and wear one on stage. I'm completely ridiculous."

"You are *not* ridiculous. You're awesome. Ah-*Maise*-ing, even." I could hear the smile in her voice. "And you're brave."

"You think so?"

"Yeah, I do. Look, you asked how I got to be so brave? You mean, how am I brave enough to wear a bikini on the beach?"

"Yeah," I mumbled. Something about the way she said it made me really embarrassed.

"I just stopped thinking of it as brave. I mean, you don't think Eva is brave for going to the beach in a bikini, do you? Or anyone else? That's what you wear to the beach. A bikini. The idea that wearing one is a brave act just because you're not a stick figure is kind of fucked up."

"Oh. Um, I'm sorry."

"No, no, I don't mean you. I mean, like, society. Most people think that way—and they're the 'nice' ones. Because fat bodies still aren't acceptable. I'm fighting to change that. A lot of people are. And I think that's brave—standing up for what you believe in. But me, just existing in my body? Wearing things that perform a function? Nah, I don't think that's brave."

I was quiet, trying to process everything she was telling me.

"But you *are* brave," she continued. "You're brave because you're scared to do this, and you're doing it anyway. Because you're going after what you want, and you're not listening to any haters—including the hater inside your own head. That takes a lot of guts. It's not something I could've done at your age."

"Really?! But you're so confident."

"I wasn't always. It's taken a lot of work for me to love myself. You're already way ahead of me."

I opened my eyes, the glue finally set on my lashes. Bess was smiling at me with a look of pride. I felt a surge of affection.

"But now you really love yourself?" I asked.

"I really, really love myself. I mean, I still have bad days—who doesn't? But I have more good days."

"Well," I said with a shaky laugh. "Here's hoping today is a good day."

"Today is most definitely going to be a good day." She stepped back and held a mirror up to my face.

I grinned at my reflection. "I think you're right."

* * *

By the time Bess and I emerged from the bedroom, Leila had arrived with the dress and cover-up she'd made for me. She was in the middle of saying something to Mum, but stopped to call out, "Woot-woo!"

Eva and Dad joined in, and Mum said, "Are you sure you don't—" but got a gentle whack from Eva sitting next to her, so she didn't finish her sentence. Instead she said, "You look lovely, Missy-May."

"Are you ready to see your dress?" Leila asked with a grin. I'd texted her the night before, when Dad and I were on our way back, and she'd replied straight away: *YAS! I knew you'd be back. You're not a Schwarzenegger fan for nothing, amirite? Your dress is ready by the way. Waiting for you.*

It made me a bit emotional, that little message. And when I finally saw what she'd made, I got *a lot* emotional. I was stunned. And a little queasy.

You know that saying—Rome wasn't built in a day? Well, neither was my self-confidence. Looking at the sheer piece of fabric that was supposed to separate my bikini body from hundreds of judgmental eyes was not what I'd call a thrill. And the dress Leila had made, while gorgeous, wasn't exactly what we'd discussed. It was a two-piece—a black crop top to go with a long A-line skirt in the bright fabric we'd bought on Boxing Day. I didn't want to be ungrateful—she'd done an amazing job, and I appreciated all the work she'd put in—but I wasn't sure I could wear it.

Eva and Bess were "oohing" and "aahing," and even Mum, who'd been doubting the whole project, said, "Wow."

Dad sniffed and said, "I like those swirly bits."

"It's beautiful," I said, reaching out to touch it. But Leila knew me better by now.

"I know what you're going to say, babe, and I don't want to hear a word of it. I have another option as backup, just in case, but I want you to try this on and tell me you don't feel like a million bucks, okay?"

I smiled and took the garment from her. "Okay. Thank you."

"My pleasure, my dear. Now go! I want to see it on!"

I emerged a couple of minutes later, still unsure. There was no full-length mirror in my bedroom, so I hadn't been able to see myself properly. I was relieved there was only an inch of skin showing between the top and the skirt, although even that was more than I'd normally share.

I crossed my fingers and tried to gauge the reactions of the others as I stepped into the lounge room. Everyone was silent for a moment.

Eva was the first to break the silence. "Oh, Maise, you look gorgeous."

"Smokin'!" Bess said. Dad gave me a thumbs-up. Leila was grinning.

And Mum...Mum had tears in her eyes. She got up and grabbed my hands. "Oh, you look absolutely breathtaking," she said, pulling me into her bedroom, where there was a full-length mirror.

As the other girls filed in behind me, I took it all in. The dress really was gorgeous. *I* was gorgeous. The top fitted my body perfectly, and the skirt made me feel like a princess (a really cool one). The inch of skin in between? It even made me feel a little bit sexy. For the first time in—well, ever—I contemplated actually liking my midriff.

I felt, as Leila had promised, like a million bucks.

I grinned and ran my hands over the smooth fabric of the skirt.

"Oh my god," I squealed in delight. "It has pockets!"

"Of course! Every girl deserves pockets," Leila said. She bit her lip. "So you like it?"

"I love it. You did a brilliant job. Thank you so, so much."

"What a talented little thing you are," Mum said, patting her on the shoulder.

Leila grinned. "Well, I'm glad you like it. Because I didn't really have a backup option."

I laughed. And in that moment, surrounded by those women, all laughing and exclaiming and embracing me, I felt more confident than I ever had in my entire life.

* * *

I'm glad I had that moment, because by the time I got changed back into more casual clothes (so as not to crumple my dress) and was in the car on the way to the hotel with Mum, Dad and about fifty bags of clothes, accessories, shoes, makeup, and other assorted tools that Mum had loaded up "just in case," I was beginning to feel sick again.

We registered and Mum helped me schlepp all my stuff backstage into the dressing room. There were a few girls in there already, fiddling in front of the mirrors. I looked down quickly, not wanting to catch their eyes. Mum was starting to unpack my bags and arrange my things.

I grabbed her hands. "Mum, go find a seat with Dad. It's cool. I got this," I said, even though I wasn't entirely sure I did got this.

Mum had tears in her eyes again. She ran a hand over my hair without actually touching it—she'd never let affection ruin a good hairdo.

"I'm so proud of you," she said, pulling me into a hug —still careful not to mess up my hair and makeup. Into my ear, she said, "That doesn't mean I've forgotten you're grounded, by the way."

I laughed, because I hoped she was joking, even though I knew better than that.

"Good luck," she said, releasing me. "We'll be cheering for you."

She blew me a kiss as she walked out the door.

A few more girls were filing in. One girl looked me up and down and smirked. Another whispered something to her friend. Probably not about me. *Don't be so self-centred, Maisie. Not everything is about you.*

Deep breaths. Deeeeeep breaths.

A pretty brunette hung up her garment bag next to mine.

"Hi," she said, with a dimpled smile. "I'm Tia." She reached out her hand for me to shake.

"Oh, um, hi," I said, awkwardly taking her hand and introducing myself.

"Is this your first pageant?" she asked.

"Is it that obvious?"

"You look kinda terrified. Don't worry, it's going to be fun. I've done this one a couple of times. Let me know if you have any questions."

I thanked her, feeling myself relax just a tiny bit. It was nice to have a friendly face in the room.

Then Tia began undressing. Looking around, I saw other girls in various states of dress/undress. A couple were already in their evening wear, which was our first section. (Evening wear in the morning? The beauty pageant industry really was revolutionary.)

"Wait. We get changed in here?" I said, trying to keep the note of panic out of my voice. Failing.

"Yeah. It *is* the dressing room," Tia said with a laugh. Standing there in her black strapless bra and undies.

Oh god. I couldn't do this.

"Where's the bathroom?" I squeaked.

When I returned, fully dressed in my gown, Tia raised an eyebrow but said, "You look great."

"Thanks, so do you," I said. And she did. She was wearing a candy pink gown with jewels down the front and an explosion of ruffles at the bottom. Leila would say it was hideous.

My phone buzzed. Speak of the devil. Leila had sent me a selfie, posing with Hannah and Jo, the words *We're here! You're going to kill it* scrawled over the top.

I sent her one back with a crown filter before noticing I had a message from Anna, too.

Good luck today x.

I sent her a *thanks* with a smiley face, and took a deep breath. I was ready.

I was adjusting myself in the mirror—making sure everything was where it should be—when chirpy Janice entered the room. "Alright, girls, today is the day! Don't you all look lovely."

My stomach twisted as I was reminded of the video

debacle. I shook my head, shaking the memory from my system. The girl standing next to me gave me a curious look, but I just smiled and looked back at Janice, focusing on the information she was delivering.

"Okay, so when you're out on stage you'll see there's a catwalk. Isn't it exciting? You're going to walk down it toward the judges at the end, do your thing, shake that booty—but not too much, keep it PG, ha ha ha—then you turn back and come off stage. Okay? Wonderful. Now, each girl should step on stage as the last girl is nearing the end of the catwalk, so you will overlap. At the end you'll all line up and walk out together. Okay? Fabulous."

She called out our names in the order we were to go on and we got ourselves in formation. I was toward the end.

I heard a "tut" behind me and turned around to see the girl who'd looked me up and down earlier. She did it again as I watched her.

"Are you alright?" I said.

She smiled a slimy Regina George smile at me. "Oh, I was just hoping the catwalk is wide enough."

Now, I had three options in that moment. I could:

a) Grab her by her hair extensions and put her in the trash.

b) Run away and cry.

c) Ignore her and rock that catwalk.

I was tempted to do a. I almost did b. That was my MO, as Anna had said.

But my dad's voice ran through my head: "*Don't give them that power. That power is yours.*"

So—spoiler alert—I did c.

I turned around and took a deep breath.

"Isn't this exciting?!" the redheaded girl in front of me said over her shoulder, jumping up and down a little as we started moving.

"Yeah, it is."

My heart thumped as we got closer and closer to the stage. My mouth was dry. Now Mum's words flashed through my mind: "*Shoulders back, chin up, smile, strut!*"

I focused on the music. On the rhythm. On the lyrics. It was Beyoncé, singing about putting love on top.

I smiled. Breathed.

My shoulders were back, my chin was up.

And I strutted.

I freaking rocked that catwalk.

I couldn't see my family and friends in the crowd, but I heard cheering off to my right.

At the end of the catwalk, I made eye contact with the judges, posed once, twice, and twirled around to strut right back again. As I passed Regina (whose real name I later found out was Vicki, like that matters) I winked.

I was absolutely buzzing.

When we all filed back on stage after the last girl had taken her turn, I got a chance to glance in the direction from which I'd heard the cheering.

I saw Mum and Dad. Eva and Bess. Leila, Hannah and Jo. All the Lees. And Beamer.

Everyone was there. Well, not everyone. My mind briefly went to Anna and a fleeting feeling of sadness came over me. Then I let the music wash back into my skin, took in the clapping of the crowd, and reminded myself this was my moment. And the people who loved me best were there.

* * *

"That was wonderful, ladies—wonderful! Now you have fifteen minutes before our next section. Chop, chop: you need to be ready on cue or you will miss out. Fabulous!" Janice whirled out of the room, leaving the smell of cheap perfume hanging in the air.

This was the moment I'd been dreading (well, one of them): the swimwear section. I went back to the bathroom to change and re-entered the dressing room in the black floral bikini Eva and Bess had given me, and the cover-up Leila had made. It too was black, with a deep V that accentuated my cleavage. The material was sheer, but not overly so. It fell to mid-thigh and covered all the areas I was most self-conscious about. When I looked in the mirror, I felt lighter. Some of the nerves that had been weighing me down dissipated. They didn't disappear completely, but I felt better. Actually, I felt pretty damn good.

As I was smoothing out my hair, smiling at myself in the mirror, Regina sidled up behind me with an obnoxious "ahem."

I looked at her reflection. She was wearing a crocheted bikini and a giant sunhat.

She crossed her arms. "Can I get some *room*? You're not the only one who needs to use the mirror, you know."

I looked down the line of girls already gathered in front of the wall-length mirror. There was still plenty of room—including space right next to me.

I smiled, and in my sweetest voice I told her so.

Her top lip drew up in a sneer. "You're taking up all the space," she spat out.

I didn't drop my smile. "Maybe if you took off that hat, you'd have more room."

"Come on, Vicki, there's room over here," a girl

called Alana said, grabbing Regina's arm and gently guiding her to the other end of the room.

"Don't worry about her," Tia said, sliding closer to me. She was wearing a strapless one-piece with a metal belt around the middle. She rested her manicured hand on my arm and smiled. "I think you're really brave, you know."

Brave. There was that word again.

Brave.

Brave. Brave. Brave.

Was I brave? Just by being there? By wearing those clothes? By going on stage? By facing my fears?

What was I really afraid of?

I was afraid of being alone.

But I wasn't alone.

I was afraid of being seen.

But I was putting myself out there to be seen.

I was afraid of being laughed at, ridiculed, made to feel ashamed.

But people did that anyway. I did that to myself.

I'd resolved to stop being ashamed.

I'd resolved to stop running and hiding.

What was I really afraid of?

Two pieces of material? A bikini? Enough.

I'll show them brave, I thought.

I pulled off the beautiful cover-up that Leila had made. *Sorry, Leila.* But I knew she'd understand.

I looked at myself in the mirror, surrounded by all those tiny girls in their tiny swimsuits.

And I saw the rolls on my belly. And the dimples on my thighs. And—*No. Stop, Maisie. Stop. Look. What else do you see?*

My eyes. My eyebrows. My ears. My hair. My fingernails. My boobs. My forearms. My smile. That bit of neck, just below my ear, next to my jaw. My midriff.

My guts.

Brave.

* * *

I tried to block out the whispers and sniggers behind me as we walked toward the stage. I had goosebumps all over. My stomach churned.

Was I about to make a huge mistake?!

Another snigger from behind spurred me on.

I tuned out those noises and tuned into the music. It was a Santigold song I really loved.

I stepped out on stage. My heart was pounding.

I breathed. Smiled. Felt tears prick my eyes.

I strutted.

Felt wobbles.

Exposed. I was so exposed.

Heard claps. Cheers.

Reached the end of the stage. Stared down the judges. Posed, posed, posed.

Twirled.

Heard whistles. Someone screaming my name.

Alive. I was so alive.

And then it was over.

My heart was racing. I was shaking.

I'd done it. I wanted to faint. I wanted to scream. I wanted to laugh and cry and shout.

And then I had to do it all over again. The swimwear section followed the same format as the evening wear—we all had to do the loop again in a line together at the end.

This time, like last time, I glanced over in the direction of my family and friends, where the loudest cheering was coming from. They were all standing up. Leila was standing on her chair. Her hands were cupped around her mouth. "Go, Maisie! Wooooo!"

I grinned. I knew she'd understand.

When I walked backstage, I went to the bathroom, and I laughed and cried and shouted. Just a little bit.

* * *

After all that, the third and final section—the talent show—should have been a piece of cake. A walk in the park. A—oh, you get the picture.

But as I stood waiting to appear on stage again my stomach was back in knots.

"Our next contestant is Maisie Martin, she's sixteen years old, and she loves movies," Janice was saying into the microphone in the middle of the stage. "Today she'll be doing—" she looked down at her clipboard "—her famous impersonations. Delightful."

As she walked off stage and I walked on she nodded to me, an insincere smile on her face.

I stepped up to the mic. "Uh, actually, there's been a last-minute change of plans. I'm going to be doing something that I've wanted to do for a long time. And I need a little help to do it."

I looked across the crowd and my gaze rested for a second on Beamer. I hoped he would understand what I was about to do.

"I'd like to invite to the stage—my sister, Eva," I said.

I moved the microphone out of the way and took my spot on one side of the stage as Eva, smiling, stepped out from the wings and stood on the other.

We were both wearing black tights and pink tops. As close to matching as we could pull together from our wardrobes in one night. And as *Dirty Dancing* as we could get.

"(I've Had) The Time of My Life" started to play,

and we both began dancing. Those long-forgotten moves—no, not forgotten. Just dormant.

I was a little rusty—Eva was far better than me—but it didn't matter. What mattered was that we were doing it together.

When I was younger, I'd always danced to lose myself. But now I felt like I was finally finding myself again. Because if watching *Dirty Dancing* had felt like coming home, then doing this dance, on stage with my sister—it was something else. Something more. It wasn't coming home—it was coming back to *me*.

As the music soared, so did I. The audience was clapping, whooping—okay, that was mainly from our own personal cheer section. But it was the best. And as the song ended, I met Eva's eyes. We were both laughing. Having the time of our lives.

See what I did there, DJ? Yeah, I'm sorry for getting cheesy. But some moments in life deserve a little cheese. And if dancing to "(I've Had) The Time of My Life" at a small-town beauty pageant with your big sister isn't one of them, then I don't know what the hell is.

* * *

You're probably wondering what happened next, right?

If this were a movie, it'd be the scene where I'm back on stage, evening gown on once again, hair and makeup as perfect as they were when the day started, waiting with the other girls to hear who would be declared *Miss Teen Queen*.

And it would be me. Overjoyed, I'd step up to accept my crown, sash and flowers, smiling and waving at the adoring crowd. Then, depending on the genre, the credits would roll, or I'd get splattered in pig's blood.

Sometimes, real life resembles the movies.

Most of the time, it does not.

Come on, DJ, you should know this by now.

This isn't a movie. This is real life.

And in real life, I stood there, back on stage, evening gown on once again, hair and makeup *almost* as good as they were when the day started thanks to touch-ups, but still looking slightly worse for wear. I was waiting with the other girls to hear who would be declared *Miss Teen Queen*.

And it wasn't me. It was Ashley, the redhead who'd been in front of me all day. She was overjoyed. She stepped up to accept her crown, sash and flowers, beaming and crying. Regina George, who placed second, stood beside her, her smile more like a grimace.

Roll credits.

Wait, no. That last bit isn't right.

There are no credits here. Because this isn't a movie.

It's my story. And it ain't over yet.

Sure, I didn't win the Miss Teen Queen title. I didn't win anything. But it doesn't matter. Not really.

Because, somehow, I still feel like I kind of won everything.

* * *

"You were spectacular, babe," Leila squealed, drawing me into a hug as soon as I emerged into the hotel lobby, dressed in my civvies again, with Mum and all my bags in tow.

Mum was trying not to cry. Or, rather, trying to stop crying. Which she hadn't been able to do for the last five minutes. She'd appeared in the dressing room to help me pack up, tears in her eyes, and the minute she saw me they spilled over.

"Sorry I didn't win, Mum," I said.

She sobbed. "Missy-May, who cares about winning? You stole the show! Those judges wouldn't know beauty or talent if it hit them with a pile of bricks."

"Amen," said Tia from behind me. She hadn't won anything either.

I laughed and hugged Mum. "Have I told you how proud I am of you?" she asked. "Because I am—so proud."

"You might have mentioned it a couple of times," I said.

Now Mum hung back, letting me talk to my friends. But mainly trying not to cry in front of everyone, I think.

Jo and Hannah were hovering behind Leila.

"You're a star," Jo said. "The best thing about the whole damn place."

"The boys said sorry they couldn't make it," Hannah said. "Cricket called." She rolled her eyes.

"Oh, no, of course. I can't believe you guys came! And stayed for the whole thing."

"Are you kidding?" Leila said. "It was great!"

"I'm sorry your dress didn't win," I said.

She snorted. "Those judges have zero taste! Who wants their endorsement, anyway? I got to see you rocking my design on that stage, and it was freaking amazing."

Suddenly Dad appeared next to me, shouting, "Eminemmmm," and enveloping me in a massive hug—the kind only dads can give.

"I'm proud of you, Em," he was saying. "So proud."

"That was incredible," Bess said from behind him.

She was standing with Eva, their arms around each other.

"Definitely a good day."

Leila tapped my hand and said, "Hey, we'll meet you back at yours, yeah? You're still doing the barbecue tonight?"

"Yeah, see you later," I said, blowing her a kiss and waving at the others.

Jimmy appeared, clapping Dad on the back and saying, "You did good, Maise," to me.

The two of them grabbed some of my bags and headed toward the car park, Mum following.

That's when I saw him. Seb.

He was standing off to the side, holding a bunch of roses.

"Mum had to take Kane and Lincoln home, they were getting kinda rowdy." He smiled. "These are for you. From all of us. To say congratulations." He handed me the roses. "You were brilliant, Maise. Way better than Chewbacca."

I laughed and thanked him. I wondered where Beamer was, but was afraid to ask.

"Beamer went back with Mum too," Seb said, as if he had read my mind.

Oh. Maybe he hadn't understood what I'd done. Maybe he was still upset about New Year's Eve. About everything.

As if reading my mind again, Seb said, "Hey, listen, about New Year's..."

I groaned. "I'm so sorry about that. I don't know what got into me."

He laughed nervously. "Nah, it's cool. I mean, I'm sorry too. I mean—this whole trip. It's been weird. Good. But weird."

"Yeah," was all I could say. I realized then that Eva and Bess had disappeared without a word. It was just Seb and I standing there in the hotel lobby.

"Hey—are you okay?" I said after a moment.

He raised his eyebrows. "Me? Yeah. Why wouldn't I be?"

"It's just with Anna—"

"Oh! Nah, I'm good. I mean—well, it was kind of a shock to find you both gone on New Year's. I've never seen your mum so angry. I swear, I thought her head was going to explode. Like, legitimately combust."

I cringed. "Yeah. I'm kind of in the most trouble I've ever been in in my life."

He chuckled, then his face got serious. "You know, I haven't heard a thing from Anna. I tried calling her a couple of times, but she never picked up. Never wrote back to any of my messages, either."

"I'm sorry," I said.

"I guess I didn't really know her, hey." Seb shrugged,

and it was like he was shaking off the bad feelings. "I'm okay, Maise. Really. You don't have to look so worried." He reached out and gave my shoulder an affectionate shove. "How are *you*? Other than, you know, being in the most trouble you've ever been in in your life?"

"Oh, other than *that,* I'm okay." I grinned. "I'm pretty great, actually."

He ran a hand through his hair. "You know...I used to have the biggest crush on you when we were younger."

My eyes widened. "No way."

"Yeah. I was always too scared to say anything. Little chicken shit."

I laughed. "Yeah? Me too."

"I'm glad we're friends again, though," he said.

"Yeah. Me too."

We stood there awkwardly for a moment. Then I said, "Could you do something for me?"

"Shoot."

I pulled a pen and—well, *you*, DJ, from my bag and tore out a piece of paper. (Soz, DJ. Hope it didn't hurt too much.) I wrote down instructions and handed them to him. He glanced at the folded up note and looked back up at me with a nod and a smile.

It was a beautiful, perfect smile.

* * *

I heard someone approaching behind me on the beach, but I wasn't ready to turn around. I stared out at the waves, thinking about how much I loved the ocean. About how long it'd been since I'd gone swimming in it. About how that was going to change.

But not right now. Right now was reserved for another kind of change.

"Maisie Martin," I heard from behind me in that lazy drawl I knew so well.

I finally turned around.

"Beamer—hey, you never did tell me your first name," I said.

He chuckled, and I felt a glimmer of hope rise in my chest. Maybe he wasn't upset with me anymore.

"That's because you never earned it."

Orrrrr maybe he was.

"Well," I said, "what if I won the movie challenge?"

"The movie challenge?" He walked toward me but veered off at the last minute to stand beside me, looking out at the water. I turned and followed his gaze. "That's why you sent a note with Seb telling me to meet you here? To talk about the movie challenge?"

I sensed some bitterness in his voice. *Come on, Maisie.*

"Well, yes," I said. "But also, no."

He looked at me then. Pierced me with his eyes. I swallowed, trying to calm my nerves.

"You left before I got a chance to talk to you today." It was a statement, but I meant it as a question.

"Yeah, I thought I'd leave it to Sebby to give you the congrats." He was watching the ocean again, rubbing his thumb along the edge of his lips. I tried not to stare. "Thought you'd appreciate it more—you know, coming from him." He sniffed, looked down, kicked some sand around.

"I appreciated that you were there," I said.

He nodded but didn't say anything.

"Beamer, about New Year's—"

He shook his head, backing up a step. "It's cool, we don't have to talk about it."

"But I want to," I said.

He let out a shaky breath. "Yeah, well, I don't."

"Can you just listen to me for a minute, please?"

He glanced at me, apparently surprised by the frustrated tone in my voice. Then he sighed, sat down in the sand, and gestured as if to say, "Well, go on."

I sat down next to him, twisting my fingers together, not sure where to start.

He picked up a stick and started drawing patterns in the sand. I followed the patterns with my eyes.

Neither of us could look at each other, it seemed.

"What you did on New Year's—" I began.

"Was really fucking awful," he said, wincing.

"What happened to letting me talk?" I asked.

He pressed his lips together.

"What you did—it was really sweet."

He snorted. "Look, I shouldn't have sprung it on you like that, alright? I mean...I knew you had a thing for Seb. I knew you were just mucking around with me. It's not your fault I fooled myself into forgetting that for a moment." He stabbed the sand a couple of times with his stick.

"But that's just it. I'd get to it if you'd let me finish. Yes, I had a thing for Seb. *Had.*"

His brows furrowed and he paused with the stick in his hand. I forged on.

"It all got so messed up. I was confused. But I've been doing a lot of thinking. And I think a part of me will always care about Seb. I mean, the Lees are family. And he was my first real crush."

Beamer's mouth twisted and that stick was stabbing the sand again.

"But that doesn't mean he'll be my last one. Not by a long shot."

The stick was still.

"Beamer, I'm really sorry for how things went

down on New Year's. But you know, if I could go back, I don't think I'd change a thing."

Back to the stabbing.

"Well, maybe the bit where I stole my mum's car and got grounded until I'm thirty...But other than that, I don't regret any of it. Because it made me realize a lot of things. Like the fact that I didn't feel the same way about Seb anymore. I'd been holding on to this fantasy for so long, and I never really stopped to question how I felt in reality."

The stick was drawing patterns again.

"But you—you made me question," I continued. "You made me question everything."

"So," Beamer said, finally looking me in the eyes, "you got any answers?"

I smiled. "A few. Here's one..." I paused. I felt like I could barely breathe as I said, "I really like you. Like, really, really *like* like you."

He dropped the stick and his hand was on my face, a smile on his lips as he brought them to mine.

And it was a good long while before he pulled back and said, "Maisie Martin, I really, really *like* like you too."

I laughed and kissed him again. And again. And again. I forgot about my promise to Mum that I wouldn't be late for the barbecue. Or maybe at that moment, I just didn't care. I was already grounded until I was thirty anyway.

Eventually, I pulled away and said, "Thank you for my poem."

Beamer's lips twisted. He looked embarrassed. "Oh yeah. The poem you thought Seb wrote."

"I can't believe how wrong I was," I said.

"What? About me? I thought you'd have it all figured out." He ran his hand up and down my arm, and I got goosebumps that had nothing to do with the temperature.

"But you know, I've been thinking too," Beamer went on. "It was the poetry that made you fall for Seb, right? Like, really fall. But I was the one who wrote it. Which means you've been a little bit in love with me all along, and you didn't even know it."

I gasped, pretending to be offended, and tickled his sides. He fell back, laughing, pulling me down with him.

After another little while I sat up and said, "This sucks."

He propped himself up on his elbows. "Thanks for the glowing review."

I rolled my eyes. "I mean, we're going home tomorrow. We live in different states! We see each other once a year."

He pulled me in to him again. "Yeah, that sucks. But, y'know, that's why Snapchat was invented." I poked him and he laughed. "And Facebook and Face-Time...and cars and planes."

He stopped talking because I was kissing him again.

"You know, we never did figure out who won the movie challenge," I said.

"Mmmmm. It's pretty obvious though."

"I won," we both said at the same time.

"I've got my scores back in my bedroom..." I said.

"Don't worry about it. I never kept score. I knew I'd win. The Rock outranks Schwarzenegger any day."

"Um, I think you'll find he does not!"

He laughed. "What would be your prize, if you won?"

"You mean now that I've won? Your first name, duh. What about you?"

He looked at me with his dark brown eyes (have I mentioned how gorgeous they are, DJ? Because I should have, a thousand times over by now), a soft smile playing on his lips, and said, "I'd ask you to dance with me."

I stood up, dusting the sand off my butt and pulling out my phone. I opened Spotify and found what I needed, turning the volume right up. I dropped the phone in the sand and reached my hand out to Beamer.

"Well, go on then," I said.

And as "(I've Had) The Time of My Life" played for the second time that day, Beamer grinned, took my hand and stood up.

"Maisie Martin," he said, pulling me in close. "Dance with me."

So I did. Right there on the beach.

And it was wonderful.

I mean, he was terrible. But it was wonderful.

We laughed a lot. Kissed a bit. Had so much fun. You might even say we had the TIME OF OUR LIVES.

(Sorry, couldn't help myself. Again. But come on, this was totally a cheese-worthy moment too.)

As the music wound down, I said, "This doesn't mean you've won, by the way."

"Oh, I don't know about that," Beamer said with a smirk. And then he leaned in close and whispered his name in my ear.

I grinned. "Don't think this means we're friends now."

"*Definitely not*, Maisie Martin." And he pulled me in for one last kiss before we joined the others.

So yeah. Life really isn't like the movies, DJ.

Sometimes, it's better.

Thursday, 9 February

Maisie,

Your dedication to your journal really is quite impressive considering your initial reluctance. There are some matters I would like to discuss with you, however. Please see me after class.

—Ms. Singh, the sadistic sumbitch

Acknowledgments

Sitting down to write these acknowledgments feels just like winning an Academy Award. Only instead of being on stage in Hollywood wearing a glamorous designer gown, I'm sitting at my desk wearing sweatpants from Kmart. Close enough.

There are a lot of people I want to thank. First of all, Jacinta di Mase and her team—the best girl gang/ agenting team I could hope for. Thank you to Danielle Binks for being such a great champion of me and my book, for speaking my language (predominantly Pacey Witter GIFs), and for being a constant source of support and advice.

Thank you to the team at Peachtree for embracing Maisie's story and giving her a home in the US. I'm particularly grateful to Jonah Heller for helping to navigate the complexities of Australian lollies versus American candy and other assorted cultural barriers.

Thank you to my Australian publishers, Pan Macmillan, for taking excellent care of me. Claire Craig, Ali Lavau, Georgia Douglas, Susan Chow, Charlotte Ree, Yvonne Sewankambo, and Hannah Membrey all contributed to giving Maisie the best possible start to public life.

Thank you to Astred Hicks for designing the perfect cover for Maisie's story. I totally judge books by their covers (I'm not even sorry), and I'm thrilled to have nothing but positive things to say about my very first one.

Thank you to Nicola Harvey, for being the very first person (other than my husband) to read Maisie's story, and who gave me all the advice, support, and praise my fragile little writer soul needed.

Thank you to Tony Broderick, Claire Low, Angela Hartman, Natalia Wikana, and Sarah Ayoub, who each read this book in the early stages and offered me generous and insightful feedback on the authenticity of my characters. Anything that isn't right is all on me—but they allowed me to pick their brilliant brains and made this book so much stronger because of it.

Thank you to Diem Nguyen for reading multiple drafts and giving me such smart and thoughtful feedback—and also for treating questions like "Is this name swoonyworthy enough?" with the gravitas they deserved. And thank you to Amanda Salles for being there throughout this whole journey—for vent sessions, cheer sessions, chat sessions and, most importantly, brunch sessions. I'm also grateful to Rebecca Finn for being a fantastic sounding board, and to Kathleen Cusack for a decades-long friendship that never wavers, no matter the distance or time between us.

This book wouldn't have been possible without so many teachers over the course of my life. But more recently, I've learned from some of the very best at the Australian Writers' Centre—Sue Whiting and Melina Marchetta. Thank you for all your wisdom and guidance.

Thank you to all the readers, writers, booksellers, librarians, and other bookish people who have embraced this book from day one. I'm also grateful to the many people in various online communities who have helped me in big ways and small.

Now we're getting to the part where the music should be playing me off—but IT'S THE MOST IMPORTANT BIT and I'm all teary.

My family. The Zampas and the Rowlands, and all my assorted in-laws—thank you for your love and support.

Adam Zampa, thank you for being the best little brother I've ever had.

Darren Zampa, thank you for being my dad and for being so proud of me.

Alison Zampa, thank you for everything. Thank you for being my earliest reader and champion, for always believing in me, and for remaining my number one fan to this day. Thank you for knowing long before I ever thought it was possible that I could write a book, and for encouraging me to reach for the stars. And, of course, a big thank you for your love of Patrick Swayze.

Chris Guillaume, thank you for being my high school sweetheart, my husband, my best friend. Thank you for waking me up at 6 AM to write, for making me smoothies in the morning and dinner in the evening and tea whenever I demanded it, for trying to make as little noise as possible when I was in writer mode, and for talking me through meltdowns of both the book and non-book variety. Thank you for being the first to read Maisie's story, for taking it seriously, and for always being supportive and proud. And thank you for reminding me to stop saying "just."

Ollie, thank you for your constant, snuggly, fluffy companionship while I write. Of course, you're a dog and will never read this, but you also don't understand most of the things I say to you and that's never stopped me.

Shirley Rowlands, I wish you could see me now. I know you would be tickled pink. I wouldn't be the person I am, or the storyteller I am, without you. Thank you for Arnold (Argen) Schwarzenegger, cups of tea, biscuits, *The Bill*, Beatrix Potter, movie marathons, secret gardens and so much more.

Lastly, thank you to anyone who reads this book. I hope you love it (no pressure!), but more than anything, I hope it helps you love *yourself* a little bit more. Just like Maisie, you deserve nothing less.

Author Q&A

This is your first YA novel. What inspired you to write it?

Initially my main aim was to write a fun summer romance—the kind I love reading. As I developed the main character, Maisie, I realized that what she really needed was a self-love story. Her insecurities with her body and some of the problems she faces as a fat girl were definitely inspired by some of my own feelings and experiences. So while I wanted her to have a really cute romance with a guy that loved her just as she is, I also wanted to give her the gift of loving herself.

Who or what inspired Maisie's character?

Maisie is definitely fictional, but some of her feelings and experiences are drawn from my own life. I had a toxic friend as a teenager and have long had a lot of insecurities about my looks, so that all went into Maisie's character. She also has my passion for pop culture—right down to her obsession with Arnold Schwarzenegger movies! But she's different from me in a lot of ways, too. I think she's braver than I am.

Where did the idea of Maisie keeping a journal come from? Have you ever kept a journal?

Maisie's journal was inspired by one I kept myself as a teen. My original draft was in straightforward first person prose, but I was struggling to move forward with it. Looking back, I realize it was because I hadn't found the right voice for Maisie. One day when I was visiting my parents, my dad forced me to clean out some of my old high school books that were gathering dust in my childhood bedroom. Amongst them I found a journal I'd had to keep for English class, and I was quite surprised to discover some of the things I'd written in it. I was a bit of a snarky teen, it turns out, and I'd made some pretty resentful comments in there—and somehow I'd still handed it in to the teacher! It gave me the idea to try writing Maisie's story in a similar journal style, and when I did something immediately clicked into place. I'd found her voice.

When you began writing, was the message of body positivity and self-love deliberate or did it evolve throughout your writing process?

It definitely evolved through the writing process. I began with the idea of a family vacation, with two boys and two girls and the complicated relationships between them. It was only when I started questioning who these characters were and why they interacted in the way they did that I came to realize how Maisie felt about her body, and that she would need some body positivity. I'm so glad the book evolved in this way, because it's a subject that's very important to me.

Young people like Maisie have been strongly affected by the culture of social media. How do you think social media has affected young people as they tackle issues of identity, body positivity, and self-esteem?

Social media puts a lot of focus on looks, so it can make it extra hard to deal with body image issues. Everyone presents an idealized version of themselves online, and it's so difficult not to compare yourself to it even though it's not reality. I think it's really important to carefully curate your feed so that you only follow people and things that make you feel good. For instance, I recently unfollowed a lot of celebs (including all the Kardashians) and instead followed a bunch of body positive Instagrammers, and it's improved my experience of the app so much! I now feel joy and inspiration when I go on there, instead of feeling more negative about myself.

Maisie struggles with body confidence, but she also learns to confront her fears and be secure in the spotlight. Have you ever done something that terrified you, like entering a pageant?

I've never entered a pageant, but when I worked at *BuzzFeed* I did appear in a video in which I tried pin-up style for the first time. Because of my insecurities I was absolutely terrified of the whole experience and almost backed out, but I ended up having the most incredible and positive day and it was this that inspired me to give Maisie a similar journey. The actual way it happens is different, but the feelings are the same.

How is writing a novel different than writing for magazines and *BuzzFeed*?

Writing a novel is totally different from my experience writing for magazines and *BuzzFeed*. For one thing, it's about 100 times more work! It's also a very different thing to construct a fictional story and create characters and build a whole new world. There's a lot of daydreaming involved. It's tough, but also wonderful fun. While I love the writing I do as part of my day job, my novel is much closer to my heart in many ways.

What is your writing routine? Do you have a favorite place to write?

When I was writing *What I Like About Me* I was working full time at *BuzzFeed*, and so I would get up every day and write for an hour before heading into work. Occasionally I would also write after work. Now I'm a freelance writer so my schedule is a bit more flexible, although on a practical level it's not much different—it's still sitting at my desk, trying to get the words down. My own desk is my favorite place to write. I can't write in public—I get distracted too easily and prefer the control and quiet I have in my own space. I also tend to "act out" the expressions of characters as I try to describe them, so privacy is important to avoid embarrassment!

Which books have had the biggest influence on your writing?

Looking for Alibrandi by Australian author Melina Marchetta was an important book to me as a teenager. I reread it constantly; it was like a faithful friend I could always turn to. It became a part of me. It's one of the reasons I really wanted to write YA—to be able to create a story that makes teen readers feel even a small portion of what that book made me feel is everything to me.

I also adore the work of Stephanie Perkins, and her YA romances were what made me sit up and think "this is what I want to write."

In terms of the craft of writing, Stephen King's *On Writing* helped motivate me to get started and keep going.

While your book has an important message of loving yourself, it also has a fun rom-com feel to it. What are some of your favorite romantic comedies? Books? Movies?

Romantic comedy is my all-time fave genre so I have many that I adore. In terms of movies: *To All The Boys I've Loved Before; Love, Simon; 10 Things I Hate About You; When Harry Met Sally;* and *The Proposal* are up there for me. In the world of books: in addition to *To All The Boys I've Loved Before* and *Simon vs. the Homo Sapiens Agenda* once again, I'm also a big fan of *Anna and the French Kiss* by Stephanie Perkins and anything by Rainbow Rowell. I love Sarra Manning and Mhairi McFarlane's works too.

If you were going on a family vacation like Maisie, where would you choose to go?

There are so many beautiful vacation spots along the coast of Australia, but I think I'd really love to travel further afield—Hawaii would be nice!

Who is the better action hero in your opinion—The Rock or Arnold Schwarzenegger?

Arnold Schwarzenegger, obviously! I am with Maisie on this one. Sorry Dwayne.

What do you hope readers take away from *What I Like About Me?*

First and foremost I hope readers enjoy *What I Like About Me* and have fun with it. I hope it makes them laugh and swoon a little, and provides a nice escape and place of comfort for them. I'd also really love if it made readers think about the way they treat their bodies and consider being kinder to themselves. In the book, Maisie starts keeping a list of the things she likes about her body, and I think that's a really simple but powerful way to show yourself a little bit of love every day. I hope readers are inspired to try it themselves!